COUNT ME IN

COUNT ME IN

A NOVEL BY

VARSHA BAJAJ

 NANCY PAULSEN BOOKS

For Aai, who taught me discipline and perseverance

CHAPTER 1

KARINA

CHRIS DANIELS AND I are like separate planets orbiting in the same galaxy.

Like the planets, we have our own paths, and I like it that way. Mine is full of photos and stories, and his is full of basketball and hyenas.

Like Venus and Earth, we are next-door neighbors. We've been in the same school since I moved to the neighborhood in third grade, but we've been in the same class only once—in fifth grade.

Then, of all the crappy karma, there he is, on the first day of seventh grade, in five out of my seven classes at Spring Hill Middle School.

How did this happen—and why?

I must've had some good karma too, because Ms. Trotter is my homeroom and social studies teacher. She is the best. She greets me with a fist bump. For real.

Ms. Trotter is flawed, though. She believes in assigned

seating. Seeing Chris sitting at the desk on my left in homeroom makes it impossible to focus. Our paths are getting dangerously close.

It makes me remember stuff from a year ago that I'd buried away, like those jeans with patchwork flowers in the depths of my closet.

Being neighbors, Chris and I have waited at the same bus stop every morning for years. He always carries some type of ball: basketball, football, or baseball. The boys play an impromptu game, as if they can't waste even those few minutes before the bus rumbles in. I typically have my nose in a book, because I have a genetic flaw that does not allow me to catch, throw, or whack a round object. Also, I don't want to be laughed at. When a girl named Emily played with the boys and flubbed a catch, they laughed all the way to school and back—for days.

It feels like survival of the most athletic on our suburban Houston streets.

And Chris was a witness to one of the worst moments in my middle-school life . . .

☆

It was in sixth grade, early in the school year. It was still ninety-eight degrees, because apparently the weather gods had not flipped the calendar from summer to fall yet.

Every ride home on the bus was a sauna, and it brought out the worst in the boys, who for some reason had turned into a pack of cackling hyenas that year.

While the rest of us fanned ourselves with notebooks or sighed in submission to the heat, they started making lists, and they were *not* harmless to-do lists.

The prettiest girls.

The bossiest girls.

The girls with the best hair. (My best friend, Ashley, made that list.)

The girls with the worst hair.

Your basic degrading grading system for girl human beings. Then Quinn, or Hyena 1, said, "Let's make a list of the girls with the hairiest arms."

Because why not, right?

Instinctively, I pulled at my short sleeves. I didn't have a sweater or cover-up, because: ninety-eight degrees.

Together, the hyenas said, "K Chops!"

Yuck! Yuck! Yuckity yuck!

Yes, I, Karina Chopra, was at the top of the list. The only one on the list. The boys thought it was so hilarious that they couldn't stop laughing long enough to name anyone else.

I glanced around through lowered lids. Some of the kids nearby pretended they had not heard, but I knew they had, because they weren't wearing earplugs, and none of them had a hearing problem.

Others were laughing.

For the briefest moment in time, like a nanosecond, I caught Chris Daniels's eye. He wiped off his grin the moment our eyes met, then looked away, because he had been seen.

Back then, I envied girls who had older brothers or sisters to protect them from bullies. Before the hairy-arms incident, I imagined that my neighbor Chris, who had grown taller and bigger, would one day be my friend and stand up for me. His older brother, Matt, was always friendly to me, but he had gone off to college a few years back.

After I saw Chris being a jerk with his friends, I realized he was not Superman. And I didn't need rescuing, anyway.

The rest of the way home, I was mad at myself for caring. Ashley, who usually sat with me on the bus, was home sick that day. If she had been there, she would have glared at the hyenas and said, "Karina, they're fools." But in a way, I was just as glad she missed it all. Who needs a witness to humiliation?

From that day forward, I wore a lot of long-sleeved

shirts to cover up my arms, even in the heat of Houston, Texas.

At first, Mom didn't notice. She and Dad were busy building their sandwich franchise. Mom had quit her nine-to-five job at an oil company a year before. Dad still had his day job as a computer systems analyst, which meant he was working twenty-five out of twenty-four hours.

Finally, one day Mom looked at me and said, "Karina, what happened to all the cute shirts that we bought for back-to-school?"

She had caught me off guard, so I blurted out the truth. "They all have short sleeves, and I need to cover up my ugly arms."

Mom and Dad exchanged one of their looks. "Oh, Karina," Mom said. "Boys can be awful. Don't let them get to you. Your arms are not ugly."

But a mother has to say that, right?

Around that same time, I was passed a note. It had my name on it in big, bold letters—**KARINA**.

I turned to see who had written to me, but everybody had their heads down.

I opened the note. The same bold letters spelled **CURRY CHOPS STINKS. GO HOME.**

When I looked back again, Hyena 1, otherwise named Quinn, was giggling.

I read the note again. This time, I took a deep breath to calm myself.

I didn't live under a rock. I knew that since 9/11, when the Twin Towers tumbled and terror came to our shores, people have looked at brown skin with suspicion. I wasn't even born then, but the stories were whispered in South Asian immigrant homes for years after. Usually, the adults tried to shield us kids. Even so, the fear seeped through closed doors and ventilation ducts.

Be careful, they said. *Be careful.*

When I was seven or eight, my older cousin told me about the Sikh American man who got shot in Arizona after the 9/11 attacks, probably because he was wearing a turban—and that alone made the murderer think, *Foreigner, terrorist.* My cousin had been telling us ghost stories. Somehow, she ended up telling us a real story that was even scarier.

I was thankful that my father and grandfather did not wear turbans, and I worried for my friends whose fathers and grandfathers did.

My parents calmed my fears; they believed in America and said we were still safe. I trusted them, because I wanted to.

It could never happen to me, I told myself. And why would it happen to me? I was like my friends and peers.

I reread the note: **CURRY CHOPS STINKS. GO HOME.**

Was I different from my friends and peers?

I knew I didn't stink. The note was Quinn's way of saying he thought I was un-American, even though I was born in Texas and so were my parents.

I remember crumpling the note very deliberately and tossing it into the trash when the teacher wasn't looking. And for once, despite my shaky hands, it fell into the basket in one determined arc, because that was where it belonged and the universe knew that. I noticed Chris Daniels watching me make that throw.

When I told my dad about the note, he let out a swear word, and I could see how upset he was. "Ignore the haters, Karina," he told me. "Keep your head down and work. My father always said that the best revenge is success. And remember, this is your country as much as it is Quinn's."

☆

Ms. Trotter asks me a question and brings me to back to class. She looks confused when I have no answer. She does not realize that I have not heard a word she said.

Chris and I don't speak to each other the rest of that first day of seventh grade. Nor do we on the bus ride home.

Today, I'd let myself be distracted by Chris Daniels.

But tomorrow will be different. I am determined to have a good year and to do well, especially in math.

Two things are definitely going to help me with that. My grandfather is moving in with us, and he is a math whiz—I will have my own personal tutor at home.

Papa coming to live with us is also great because it means I won't have to go to the sandwich store after school. I'll get a break from slicing cucumbers and tomatoes, and I'll have more time for my photography.

In the evening, I borrow Dad's Canon and stroll around the neighborhood, taking pictures. I need to submit my best photograph for an art gallery competition, later this fall, and I'm still shooting.

I can already see my photograph hanging on the gallery's perfect walls, bathed by a spotlight. I can hear the applause. I can smell the wine and cheese. Will they have sparkling cider for the underage exhibitors?

Yes, it is going to be a very good year.

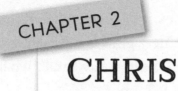

CHAPTER 2

CHRIS

AWKWARD.

Karina Chopra is in five out of my seven classes this year.

[She and I haven't exchanged a word in like a year or something. *Daniels,* I tell myself, *she thinks you're one of the mean dudes.* I hate that.]

Ms. Trotter is all over her. "It's so good to have you in my class," she tells Karina, beaming.

Karina is all smiles. Like nobody has told that girl the basic rule of social survival. Be cool when an adult, especially a teacher, gushes over you. Instead, Karina is all giggly, and then they fist-bump. Like they're besties!

But Karina doesn't seem to care what people think. She's got her nose in a book at the bus stop every morning. And every couple of days, she has a new book.

(I'd like to say something to her, to be able to tease her in a good way, but the memory of stuff that happened at the beginning of middle school stops me.]

That day, on the bus, the guys started making lists. Dumb lists. The prettiest girls, the bossiest, etc. Those lists are not my thing. I never say much when the guys do stuff I don't think is funny.

Then Quinn had the bright idea of making a list of the girls with the hairiest arms.

I groaned. Nothing good would come out of this, I knew.

"K Chops is the queen of hairy arms," he declared, and then he yukked it up as if it was the funniest thing ever.

I looked across the aisle right when Karina was looking my way. She gave me a look that said, *I feel sorry for you.* After that, she kept a poker face, opened her backpack, took out her book, and read the whole way home.

I wish I had said something. If only I knew Karina better and could explain things. I wish I had told her that with her brown eyes and big smile, she should have been on the list of prettiest girls.

That evening, I called my brother, Matt, who was away at college.

I told him about how cool it was to be on the basketball team and how I'd scored. And then I told him about the bus and Karina, because it had bothered me all day and Matt is the best listener in the whole world.

Matt groaned. "That's ugly, dude."

I could also count on him to understand. *Ugly* was correct.

"What'd you do?" he asked.

What could I have done? I had asked myself that question. I was sitting on the bus with the guys from the basketball team, and I had only waited forever to be able to sit with them—to be one of the guys. If I had said something at the time, what price would I have had to pay?

The middle-school bus is a monster that no one has slayed, as far as I know. Being quiet—biting your tongue, swallowing your thoughts and words—is how you survive. So far, those tactics have worked for me.

"Doing the right thing is hard," he said when I was silent. "But, Chris, at least you *know* what is right and wrong."

I did know the difference, but was that enough? Did I need a new game plan?

"I'll be home in a few weeks, Chris. Hang in there, okay? We'll shoot hoops together and talk."

Since that day, Karina hasn't talked to me.

To make things even worse, around that same time, Quinn passed Karina a nasty note. I remember watching her face crumple when she opened it. Then she tossed it in the trash when Mrs. Clay wasn't looking.

All through that class, I kept thinking about the note. What could Quinn have said? There was no way for me to concentrate on word problems with fractions. At the end of the class, after everyone left, I dug through the garbage and found the tightly balled note. I smoothed the paper and read it.

CURRY CHOPS STINKS. GO HOME.

At first, I didn't even understand it. Quinn wanted Karina to go home in the middle of the day? Why did he call her Curry? And she didn't stink.

Then it sunk in how he was insulting her.

I called good old Matt again. What would I do without him? I felt bad for anyone who didn't have Matt as a big brother. When I told him what happened, Matt was silent for the longest time.

"You there?" I asked.

"Quinn is a small-minded squirt," he said.

The next day, I was already feeling pretty angry toward Quinn when we were put on opposing teams during a basketball game in PE. Each time Quinn ran toward the basket to score, I was a defensive wall and he couldn't score at all. He got angry and crashed into me, making me fall.

"Trash play," I yelled at him. "What's your problem anyway, dude?"

Quinn gave me a funny look, but I didn't care. I was mad—about a lot of things.

Why was it so hard to do the right thing?

☆

Now, on the first day of seventh grade, I remember that moment. I wish that Karina had been there at that basketball game when I told Quinn off. Too bad girls have separate PE. Could I maybe reach across the aisle and tell her that? A year after the fact? Nah! She'd think I'd lost my marbles.

CHAPTER 3

KARINA

ON LABOR DAY weekend, Papa moves in. We invite all the relatives to celebrate.

When my grandfather puts on his red silk tunic, I know it's going to be a good party. He saves that one for weddings and festivals. He hums a Bollywood song as he cleans and polishes his glasses. To me, they look like Harry Potter glasses. To him, they are Gandhi glasses.

It took a while for my parents to persuade him to leave California and live with us. After Grandma passed, Mom and Dad called him every single day and badgered him to come.

This is how it finally went down to get him to agree:

Mom said, "We have our hands full with the franchise, and we may want to expand. We really need your help in raising Karina."

That argument clinched the deal.

"If my granddaughter needs me, I will come," Papa replied.

Hence the party.

Part of me is worried about sharing the upstairs with Papa. He will be in the spare room, which I had been using to spread out all my pictures and stuff. My room would not have won any neatness awards before, and now, with all my pictures in it, it's really cramped. Gah!

I know Mom is also worried about having Dad's father moving in. She wonders if he'll expect her to be the dutiful Indian daughter-in-law, old country style.

I overheard them discussing it the other night. If I sit on the stairs, I can hear most of what they say when they talk in the living room. They might not like that, but sometimes I need to do it to stay on my toes.

"Do you think Papa will expect me to cook Indian food every night?" Mom asked.

"I hope not," Dad said. "We make do with takeout from the store, and he'll have to as well."

"What if he thinks I'm an awful daughter-in-law?" she wailed.

"He won't," Dad said. "How could he?"

Mom replied, "I just want things to go smoothly, you know?"

I know that's what we all want. I start to wonder what people will think of Papa's accent, but I brush the thought aside and focus on the benefits of Papa moving in.

Especially that I can chill at home more, because there will be someone here to keep me company.

Dad is in the living room, hanging the WELCOME TO HOUSTON, PAPA! sign I made. And Mom is running around the house, straightening things that are already straight. She had the chicken tikka masala and naan catered but took the day off yesterday to make the vegetables and salads.

She yells for Dad. "Babe, have you tasted the aloo? Is the salt okay?"

He and I tasted the potatoes a few hours ago, and we both certified that the salt was fine. Mom has clearly lost her mind.

"Babe?" she calls again. Dad and I roll our eyes.

Then she stops in her tracks and finally notices how I am dressed. "Aww!" she says when she sees me in the traditional Indian ghagra choli. I beam. I am feeling it too. I posted a picture with the caption OOTD— outfit of the day—for my friends. The skirt is full and to the floor, and has a green-and-yellow paisley print. The solid-yellow blouse is fitted and shows a sliver of tummy. I have looped the scarf that matches the skirt around my neck.

"Now all you need are some earrings!" Mom says, giving me a hug. "Go and find some from my jewelry box."

Family arrives within minutes of each other, like they'd planned the chaos, including Mom's brother; Raj Uncle and Lindsey Aunty and their kids; and Dad's sister and her kids. Everyone is talking over one another. I grab a plate of samosas and race my cousins upstairs to play the Wii.

An hour later, our house is bursting at the seams with hugging people—and music, food, and laughter. I hear guests welcome Papa repeatedly, tell him how happy they are that he has moved here, and invite him over for a meal. Papa must be beaming.

When we come down for lunch, the tension has slipped off Mom's shoulders, or maybe she shrugged it off. Now she is relaxed—and she grins when the pulsating beat of the bhangra music starts.

My cousins and I giggle as all the grown-ups get on their feet. I'm not sure how it happened, but it has become a dance party. I have a theory, though: I think it's the call of Papa's magical red silk tunic.

Someone eggs Papa on. "C'mon. It's your party. You have to join us."

Papa is the center of attention with his white mane and his big laugh.

My cousin whistles.

Mom claps, and her foot taps.

Papa walks over to me. I want to run and hide. I am

not the best dancer, but when Papa has both his hands outstretched, how can I refuse? Papa can move, even with his arthritis.

Now everyone is clapping to the beat. I twirl, and so does my skirt.

Midtwirl, I freeze.

I see the strangest thing.

What? How?

Chris Daniels, my next-door neighbor, is in the middle of my living room. Chris Daniels, the boy who is friends with the hyenas, just saw me spinning in my dressed-up Indian outfit.

I want the ground to split and swallow me.

My raised hands fall and tug my blouse over my exposed middle. I miss my footing and stumble right into Chris. He catches me. That's how I know he's not a hologram.

"I knocked. I . . . I rang the doorbell," he stutters.

Of course he did. But there was no way we could have heard over the music rocking the Chopra house.

Chris points to the front door. "My dad wants to talk to your dad," he says.

I nod and go to find him, wondering what on Earth his father would want to say to Dad.

I tug at Dad's shirt and point to Chris, telling him Chris's dad is outside.

Dad walks out. Chris and I follow. Before Dad can close the door, Papa steps out too.

Chris's dad is pacing outside. He looks like he inhaled a steam engine.

"I can't pull out of my house, and I'm running late," he says, pointing at the car blocking part of his driveway.

He could have said hello. He always seems to be in a big hurry, too busy to chat.

I see Dad take a deep breath. "I'm sorry!" he says calmly. "Give me a minute, and I will have the car moved."

Dad leaves to find the owner of the car.

Then I hear Chris say, "See you in school, Karina."

That surprises me. We have never "seen" each other in school before, and I was not expecting our orbits to collide.

CHAPTER 4

CHRIS

LAST NIGHT, I left a letter from my math teacher on the kitchen counter. I knew it would make the gray clouds gather. As predicted, it's a stormy day inside the house even though it's bright and sunny outside.

The strategy was top-notch. They would come home after dinner with their friends and be in a happy mood, and they would see the letter. They would have time to sleep on it. Mom would calm Dad down after he saw the note, which said:

> *Dear Mr. and Mrs. Daniels,*
>
> *I worry that Chris may not be in the right class. We should discuss his math abilities and aptitude.*
>
> *Sincerely,*
> *Mrs. Hubbard, 7th Grade Math*

My last worksheet is attached. A letter *D* is etched in red. It's early in the school year, just Labor Day weekend, too early to start dealing with the math beast. But the math teacher doesn't agree with me; she thinks problems should be "nipped in the bud."

I was struggling. Finding the value of x was as impossible as finding the socks that got lost in the laundry every week. Maybe the washing machine had the socks and the x answers.

When I enter the kitchen, Mom is drinking coffee, and Dad is trying to fix a lopsided blind by pulling on it.

He yanks.

The blind responds by now tilting at a sharp angle. Dad swears.

Mom notices me and says, "Good morning, sleepyhead. We saved you some food."

Dad yanks again. If it doesn't work once, you should always try the failed method again.

Then he sees me.

"Need to talk about this," he says, picking up the worksheet and waving it around.

"Bill!" Mom says. "Give the boy a chance to eat."

Dad yanks for a third time. The blind is now at an even sharper angle. He cusses again. "I'm going for a shower and then to the mechanic. The car's making a strange sound. Last thing we need. They'll say the transmission is about to die and charge thousands of dollars. Last thing we need."

When Dad's stressed, he repeats himself.

As he walks away, he says, "Chris, your math grade has to improve."

"Yes, sir!" I say.

"Chris, honey," Mom says, "maybe you should start going to the after-school tutorials. Your aunt says they really helped Tim."

"Or maybe I need to forget about algebra and drop down to the easier math class," I say, frustrated.

"Chris, look at me," she says. "Can you honestly say that you've tried your very best?"

She has a point, but I ignore her question. "Maybe Dad needs to go for some anger-management classes," I mumble.

"Chris," she says. "Dad is stressed about work. There were more layoffs at his company last week. He's worried. I'll talk to him."

Mom always makes excuses for Dad's irritability. Wish she'd make similar excuses for my math grades.

Dad heads out while I'm still in the kitchen, eating. Slowly, I take one bite of waffle and another of eggs—alternating sweet and salty, the way I like it.

A few minutes later, Dad returns. "A car's blocking the driveway. The neighbors must be having a party. There are cars lining both sides of the street. Chris, go tell them to move that car."

"Why me?" I say. "I barely know them."

"Isn't the kid in your class?" asks Dad.

"Yeah, but she doesn't even talk to me."

"Go! Go," he says.

Karina's family has lived next door for years, but my parents hardly talk to them either, except to say good morning. Dad believes that just because you live next door to someone, it doesn't mean you have to be friends. When they first moved in, Mom thought of trying to get to know Mrs. Chopra, but she never seemed to find the time to go over and say hello.

I quickly change into shorts and a T-shirt, and run across the yard.

Cars are parked all down the street and into the cul-de-sac. Someone has squeezed their car into a space outside our house, but it blocks our driveway enough that backing out is impossible.

I ring the doorbell and wait.

Dad's in his car, watching impatiently.

I ring the doorbell again. Embarrassing.

No answer. I can hear the party inside.

I ring the doorbell for the third time and try not to look over at Dad. I can feel his foot tapping.

I count—*1-2-3-4-5-6-7-8-9-10*—and turn the knob on the front door.

On the outside, our houses are built of the same bricks and siding. Same windows and door. Same oak trees in the front yard. Same front doors. They are like two chocolates in a box.

But on the inside, they have different centers.

There are at least fifty people milling around. I stand in the foyer unnoticed, gaping. How am I supposed to find Karina?

Some of the women are wearing bright Indian clothes, and a few of the men wear turbans. I'll have to ask Matt why—or Google it.

The music pulsates, but the lyrics are in a language I don't recognize. And it's loud. No wonder they didn't hear the doorbell.

A homemade banner says WELCOME TO HOUSTON, PAPA!

Who is Papa?

I remember that Dad is waiting in the driveway. I need to find Karina's dad. Fast.

I take a few steps into the living room, and I see her. She is dancing with an older man. His loose, long shirt is as red as Superman's cape.

As she twirls, Karina's skirt is like a floating halo around her feet.

She turns and sees me.

Karina stumbles. I don't blame her. I would lose my footing too if I suddenly saw *her* in *my* living room. She collides straight into me. We almost land on our butts, but I manage to step back, find my balance, and steady us.

"I knocked. I . . . I rang the doorbell," I say.

She looks stunned, as if she doesn't understand.

"My dad wants to talk to your dad," I say.

"Oh!" she says. "Okay."

Within minutes, Karina finds her dad and they step outside with me.

Dad is now pacing outside. I wish he had stayed in his car. I wish that he had taken a deep breath and calmed down while he waited.

The older man in red, who must be Karina's grandfather, steps out too.

Dad points to the car blocking our driveway. He sounds annoyed when he tells them he's running late.

I want to evaporate into thin air.

Karina's dad apologizes. He says he'll have the car moved in a minute and runs back inside to get the driver.

Dad notices the older man and nods in greeting before he walks off to wait in his car.

I want to tell Karina that my dad's having a bad morning, but that would be weird.

Karina introduces her grandfather. "He just moved here from California," she says.

I shake his hand.

Daniels, I tell myself, *you gotta make up for your father's lack of friendliness with a smile that splits your face.*

"See you in school, Karina!" I blurt out as they leave.

CHAPTER 5
KARINA

IT'S BEEN ALMOST a week since the party. A week since Chris Daniels was in my living room. Every day since then, he smiles at me. It's a hesitant smile, which I respond to with another hesitant smile.

He still sits on the bus with the hyenas. I imagine it would be hard to break from the pack—on Animal Planet, they said if a hyena tries to leave his pack, sometimes the others will literally tear him apart and have him for dinner.

I don't want Chris Daniels to be eaten alive, even though the hyenas did laugh at me when Quinn made that crack about my arms. But I guess I should let that go. First of all, I don't care anymore—I've learned to like my arms the way they are. And second of all, it was over a year ago. We've both grown since then. Papa always says, "Let bygones be bygones. They are too heavy to carry around."

Speaking of Papa, in the week he's been with us, he's transformed our house.

I shouldn't be surprised. I remember how perfect he and Grandma kept their house in California, inside and outside. The lawn was always mowed, weeds were too afraid to grow, clutter never piled up, and faucets did not dare to drip.

Dad remembers Papa always puttering around fixing things, but he figured that Papa had probably slowed down in his seventies. Wrong! He's still like the Energizer Bunny. Going! Going! Going!

Last Monday, Papa made matar paneer with home-made paratha, and it was so good that Mom, Dad, and I couldn't stop eating till every last bit was gone.

"Since Grandma died," he said, "I taught myself to cook from YouTube videos."

I remembered him also telling me that during one of our weekly Skype chats. I'd thought he meant he could make some pasta or eggs.

That evening, I overheard Mom saying she feels guilty that Papa is cooking for us. But Dad says it's okay, because it makes my grandfather happy. I think Papa keeps busy because when he sits still by himself, he feels lonely.

"Your grandma and I were married for forty-five years and never spent more than a few days apart," he tells me. "We loved being with each other."

I cannot even imagine what that is like. I see him look wistfully beyond the trees in the backyard, as if he can see Grandma waiting for him on the horizon.

And so he keeps busy, hopping from one thing to another—polishing this, scrubbing that, repairing this, replacing that, reorganizing this, decluttering that.

Until on Thursday, we cannot find cereal or computer paper or scissors, and I find Mom sitting at the table in the kitchen, intently coloring a mosaic picture of a palace. The coloring book was a checkout-line purchase to help her de-stress. I have never seen her use it before.

Mom whispers to me, "Today, Papa replaced the broken slats in the fence."

"The fence between our house and Chris's?" I whisper back.

Why are we whispering when Papa is out in the yard? I think we worry that he can be everywhere at once.

"Yes!" Mom says. "He didn't ask them or anything. He got into the car, got what he needed at the store, and did the job."

She groans.

He is mending fences, like Chris and I are. We even ended up as partners in English class yesterday. We will see how that goes.

"Hopefully they won't mind," I say. "Maybe they will even be happy."

Mom picks up a red pencil and colors. "I don't know. Dad said Mr. Daniels was a bit intense when they spoke the day of the party."

Yes. He was that. I now understand Mom's stress—who knows what Mr. Daniels will say. Papa should have waited till we talked to the neighbors before he took on a repair job.

"So what are you going to do?" I ask her.

"Dad thinks we should go over and explain things to them," she says. "I also think Dad needs to talk to Papa about telling us before he starts on projects."

"Good luck with that," I say, and Mom shows me that her fingers are crossed.

☆

Later, in the evening, the doorbell rings. I peek through the peephole.

"Mom," I call out in panic. "It's Chris's mom."

Mom is all flustered. "Whoa! She beat us to it. I wish your dad was here."

We invite Mrs. Daniels in. She seems as nervous as us, and she's clutching a checkbook.

"Mrs. Daniels, please come in. I've been meaning to stop by, but . . ." Mom's voice trails off.

"Thank you," Mrs. Daniels says. "We noticed that someone repaired the fence between our houses."

"My father-in-law," Mom tells her. "We didn't know he was planning to do that. If we had, we would have said something before—"

"My husband has always meant to fix it too," Mrs. Daniels says.

The conversational dance is as awkward as a hippo dancing with a gazelle.

"We'd like to pay our portion of the repair work," Mrs. Daniels says.

"Oh no! No!" Mom gets as red as a beetroot. "Please!"

Mrs. Daniels blushes too but insists. "We can't not contribute our share."

"We should have asked your permission. After all, that fence belongs to us both," says Mom.

"Which is precisely why we should share the cost of the repairs," Mrs. Daniels says.

Finally, Mom gives in. She promises to figure out the cost and let her know. Whew!

☆

At dinner, Dad tells Papa that maybe next time they should ask the neighbors before taking on any more fence-mending. Dad stares at his plate as he talks. I have never heard him mumble so much.

It must be hard to discipline your parent. I can't

imagine telling Dad what to do someday. I want to giggle so badly that I stuff my face instead and almost choke.

Papa looks at Dad as if he is speaking a foreign language. "Why? It needed fixing. I am doing everyone a favor."

Dad looks over at Mom. She is no help. Her look says, *Don't look at me. He's* your *dad.*

After Mom and I clean up, I spread my homework out on the dinner table. Mom sits next to me to work on her stress-free coloring, and Papa is at the other end, drinking his tea. He looks hurt and is staring out through the trees.

I hand my mother a stack of school announcements. She scans them, and then she jumps to her feet and waves one of the papers in the air.

"Papa!" she says. "Look at this. Karina's school needs volunteers to tutor math."

Papa takes the flyer and reads it. "I will volunteer."

"My thought exactly!" Mom declares.

"Wait a minute—what?" I say.

But, really, no one is listening to me. Why should they? It's only my school.

"You are so good at math," Mom says. "Jay said you helped him all the time growing up. Even with calculus."

Papa is beaming. Mom looks like she's tamed a lion.

"This is perfect," says Mom. "You will help so many kids."

Mom and Papa high-five each other. Mom immediately emails the contact on the flyer and says Papa will come on Tuesday.

It is decided, sealed.

"Isn't this great?" Mom says. "You can go with Papa and do your homework while he tutors."

I fake-smile, but I am worried. Papa with his lilting accent is unmistakably an immigrant from India, even though he has lived in this country for fifty-some years. My parents, on the other hand, were raised here. They speak like every other parent I know. They even say "y'all."

I pray that none of the hyenas will be in Papa's tutorials, because who knows what they might say.

I especially pray that Quinn is not in the tutorial session. I already know what he would say.

CHAPTER 6

CHRIS

MOM HAS SIGNED me up for math tutorials after school on Tuesdays and Thursdays. Dad and she both agree that I need to work harder before they decide to let me drop down. Then they tell me I can't play basketball till I start doing better at math.

That's how I know they mean business.

The rest of the team is rooting for me. When I tell Coach, someone says, "Why do you need algebra? You have the moves."

If only my mom had heard that!

If Matt was home, I wouldn't need tutorials, because he could teach me is what I'm thinking as I walk to the empty cafeteria after school on Tuesday.

I take a bite of my granola bar and shower myself with crumbs.

"Welcome to tutorials," Mrs. Taylor says, her chipper voice greeting me like she's welcoming me to a game or something.

"Thanks," I mumble.

There are a handful of kids here already. I survey the room to decide where to sit when I spy a man cleaning his round glasses. He's not wearing a red tunic shirt like the other day, but a regular button-down shirt. It's Karina's grandfather, and I wonder, *What's he doing here?*

I don't have to wonder for long, as I hear Mrs. Taylor approach. "Chris," she says. "I have the perfect teacher for you." Her hand on my back guides me to Karina's grandfather. "Meet Mr. Chopra."

Daniels, I tell myself, *short of making a run for it, there is nothing you can do.*

Really, what were the odds that he would be my math tutor? And the last thing I need is smarty-pants Karina knowing how much help I need with math.

"Chris!" says Mr. Chopra. "Are you the boy who lives next door? I would be happy to help."

I mumble a thank-you, and that's when I notice Karina doing her homework at one of the tables across from us, pretending like she doesn't know her grandfather or me.

Great. Just great.

She smiles at me and shrugs.

"Sit! Sit, beta," Mr. Chopra says.

I'm not sure what *beta* means, so I don't sit.

Karina understands my confusion and explains that *beta* means "son" but that you can call a daughter "beta" too.

"I get it," I say. "Like Coach sometimes calls us 'son.'"

Mr. Chopra and I sit, and Karina goes back to her work.

"I was terrible at math when I was your age," Mr. Chopra says. "My older brother taught me by stealing my sesame candy."

Seeing my puzzled look, he says, "My brother would pile my candy between us. Each time I got an answer wrong, he would eat one. Some days, he ate it all. I learned fast—if only to save my candy." He laughs.

I find myself telling him about my older brother, Matt. Then I tell him that I need to learn fast too, because unless I have at least a C, Mom and Dad won't let me play basketball.

Mr. Chopra says, "We cannot have that. Basketball is important."

"It is?" I say hesitantly.

"I love basketball," he says. "I used to enjoy seeing the Lakers play when I lived in California."

My eyes pop. "Sweet!"

He tells me that he saw Magic Johnson dunk from the nosebleed seats back in the day.

That's when I find out that he knows about all the Lakers games and stats, and that we could talk ball all day. He says now that he has moved to Houston, he will have to root for the Rockets too.

He gets a gleam in his eyes. "That's enough chitchat. We have to get you back on that team."

Then Mr. Chopra decides to rake me over the coals. He wants to see how much I know and don't know. "Chris, I like you, so I have to test you."

"Why?" I ask.

"In math," he says, "the concepts build on each other. If the foundation is weak, the building will collapse." He says this in a tone that makes me wish I had listened to all my teachers from kindergarten on.

Mr. Chopra starts scribbling problems on a piece of paper.

I look around me. Mrs. Taylor guards the entrance. There is no escape.

I catch Karina's eye. A sound escapes her lips, and I'll be darned if it isn't laughter.

I raise my eyebrows at her, and she mouths, *Sorry. Can't help it.*

Karina Chopra, I want to say, *I am not amused!*

Mr. Chopra looks up at her. "Karina, go drink some water," he says.

"I'm okay, Papa," she answers, all innocent, and buries her head in her book.

I try to focus when Mr. Chopra hands me the sheet. Lots of the problems look like fast facts I memorized in elementary school. For real. This is so embarrassing. What if I get an easy one wrong?

Mr. Chopra says, "Are you ready, Chris?"

As ready as I'm ever going to be to face a firing squad where the bullets are math problems. I nod.

Two hundred million years later, Mrs. Taylor announces it is time to leave.

On the way out, Mr. Chopra asks, "When is your next quiz?"

"Thursday," I tell him.

"What?" he says, and stops in his tracks. "Thursday? But you are not ready, and I cannot have a student of mine do poorly on a test."

"Don't worry. I'll be prepared for the one next week," I say. "If I suddenly do too well, Mrs. Hubbard will think I'm cheating."

"Nonsense," Mr. Chopra says, and brushes me off. "You will come to my house after school tomorrow. We will work hard. You may not get an A, but you will not fail."

I explain that to my puzzled parents when I tell them that I am going next door on Wednesday evening.

Matt thinks it's great I am getting help. "Dang, Chris, you might become an engineer after all," he says, and then he sounds like a witch as he laughs and laughs.

I hang up on him.

I had never gone to Karina's house in all the years that she has lived here, and now I was going there twice in a little more than a week!

☆

I end up with a C for "commendable" on my math quiz, rather than an F for "fried." I also have a new friend in Mr. C.

He high-fives with so much energy at our next session that my hand tingles. "Chris," he says, "now we move on to the solving of equations."

Before he starts the session, he places a card holder between us. The card has *FOCUS* written on it, in bold red capital letters. Is Mr. C hypnotizing me?

"Miracles never cease," Mom says when my next decent grade comes in. "You find a way to thank Mr. Chopra. You say 'thank you,' you hear?"

Even Dad is grateful. Now when he sees Mr. Chopra outside weeding or something, Dad slows down, waves, and says hello. It makes me happy to see him act friendly.

I start going to Karina's house regularly, to ask Mr. C questions or hand him work to review, but she's rarely around. Her grandfather says she's out on a walk, or taking pictures, or at her friend's place. He tells me that she wants her photographs to be selected by an art gallery, that she takes beautiful pictures that she posts on the internet. I start to follow her photo feed so I can see them.

I'm not scared before the next test. Mr. C shows me how to breathe deep so I don't feel anxious. He texts and reminds me to eat breakfast the morning of the test. When I see the questions, some of them are familiar and I know I can handle them. I get a C+.

When I show Mr. C my grade, he yells, "You did it!"

He gives me a bag of Peanut M&M's. He remembered that they're my favorite. I rip open the bag and share them with him.

"We did it!" I say with my mouth full.

CHAPTER 7
KARINA

"OUCH! OUCH!" I say.

Ashley drops the brush in horror. "What? What?"

"That hurt," I whine.

"I'm sorry," Ashley says. "But it's not easy, and you keep moving your head."

Ashley is separating my tangled hair into sections so she can weave a French braid. I am reading the instructions aloud.

We take a break after Ashley ties three lopsided ponytails to save the painfully separated segments of my hair. One of the ponytails looks like a fountain on the top of my head. Now *that* is a nutty look. I stick my tongue out and take a selfie.

The bowl of Chex Mix has a few mouthfuls left. "Want them?" Ashley asks, pointing to my favorites.

That's how good a friend she is. She knows I search out the breadsticks. Ashley likes the rye chips. We are perfect for each other.

"Hey, how's the tutoring thing going?" Ashley asks. "I can't believe your grandfather has to work with Chris Daniels!"

"Yes," I tell her. "He's over here all the time."

Ashley shakes her head in disbelief. "Poor you. I hope he's gotten nicer. I'm still mad about that horrible list back in sixth grade!"

Although Ashley hadn't witnessed my humiliation that day, I ended up telling her every detail later, and she got properly ticked off at the hyenas.

Now I tell Ashley about how weird it is to see so much of Chris. "It's like I can't get away from him," I say.

"Are you going to become friends or something?" Ashley's eyes are as wide as quarters.

"Papa and Chris are friends," I say. "We're not— probably because when he comes over, I hide out in my room."

Ashley laughs and starts braiding my hair again. "You don't still think boys have cooties, do you?"

"No, I guess we have moved past the cootie stage," I say. "And that stuff on the bus happened a while ago."

"It did," she says. "Starting middle school feels like ancient history."

"We've grown, and I think he has too," I say. "It's good to give people second chances, right?"

"Sure, that makes sense," says Ashley. "I gave Brussels sprouts a second chance, and now I love them."

"So are you comparing Chris to a vegetable?" I say.

Ashley laughs and drops a section of hair. "No more talking about Chris Daniels," she says, "or we'll be braiding till tomorrow. Don't turn, don't move, and don't talk. I need to focus."

I obey. On the wall in front of me is the Valentine's Day card that Ashley made for me in third grade.

Our teacher that year had given us blank pieces of construction paper and told us to create heart drawings for anyone we loved.

At the end of class, Ashley showed me her artwork. She had drawn a tree.

"Psst!" I whispered. "You were supposed to draw a heart."

"I did," she said. "Look closely." And when I did, I noticed that each leaf on the tree was a perfect green heart.

"Oh, Ashley," I said. "That is beautiful."

"I made it for *you*," she said.

We've been best friends ever since.

Now Ashley says, "I'm done. Your hair looks gorgeous."

She holds a mirror behind me so I can look at the braid.

It is amazing—just like my friendship with Ashley. Our lives are braided together like strands of hair.

CHAPTER 8

CHRIS

MR. C IS a genius at teaching math. Somehow when he teaches me fractions, they all make sense. It helps that he uses food to get his points across. We pull apart orange sections, cut apples, and even make a pie. *Fractions with Food*—that should be a TV show.

Mr. C says lots of people are hands-on learners—that's true for me. And all of a sudden, like magic, I understand how fractions and ratios and percentages relate.

"Chris," Mr. C tells me, "we are making your foundation stronger."

"Phew," I say. "Because my building was sure gonna collapse!"

We are a good team, Mr. C and I. I like making him laugh, and he likes feeding my stomach and my brain.

☆

We are taking a break, staring at a computer screen, when a voice behind us asks, "What're you watching?"

I jump.

It's Karina.

I've come over so many times when Karina's never around that I've gotten to thinking about it as Mr. C's house instead of hers.

"I found a video of the best Lakers players of all time," I say. "You know how your grandpa loves the Lakers."

She lifts her eyebrow. "You don't say."

Duh, I'm telling her stuff about her own grandfather. But Karina's cool about it. She gets a bowl of Goldfish and then sits down to join us.

I never thought Karina Chopra would want to watch a basketball highlights reel, but what do I know?

Mr. C can't stop smiling. He's into it like it's a live game at the Staples Center.

"Ew!" Karina says. "Those old uniform shorts were as short as Daisy Dukes."

"They are short shorts for sure," I say, and we all crack up—and we agree the longer shorts look way better.

Every few minutes, Mr. C pauses the video because he has a story to tell, sometimes about a foul ball, other times just about a delicious hot dog topped with melty cheese. And once about seeing Magic Johnson score a gazillion points in a game.

Mr. C gives me a high five when the video is done. "Chris, you picked a good one. Thank you!" He says it like I'd just given him a present.

"Anytime," I tell him.

I decide I'm going to find more old videos for him.

Before I go, Karina surprises me by asking for a favor. "Chris, I need help choosing a photo for the tween competition at the gallery," she tells me. "I've shown them to a few people, but I could use another opinion."

Karina wants my opinion? On her photographs? Has the Earth stopped spinning on its axis?

"Sure," I stammer.

I help Mr. C clear the dining room table, and when Karina returns, she arranges the photos there.

"You can look now," she says when they are all spread out. "The theme for the competition is 'Home.'"

Karina has awesome pictures of all kinds of homes, big and small. I zero in on one of a turtle in its shell and another one of a really cool tree house.

Mr. C slowly picks up one after another and stares at each one.

"Wow!" I say. "These are great. You took them all with your cell phone?"

"Some," she says. "But I have a Canon that my dad lets me borrow."

"That's my fave," I say finally, pointing to one of the night sky. "If I stare at it, I feel like I'm being sucked into a galaxy far, far away. But it's cool to be reminded it's our home too, *our* galaxy."

Mr. C lifts it up. "There is Venus shining bright. Karina—I like that. And I also like the turtle. I love how every detail of his shell is clear. Whatever you choose will be perfect. They are all good."

"You're saying that because you're my grandfather," she tells him.

"No. I say it because you are good," he says. "One day your photographs will be in a gallery—and, Chris, one day you will get an A."

I like that Mr. C is ambitious for us. It feels good to have him pulling for me and Karina—I just wish we were as confident.

"Papa," Karina says, "you remember the cake Grandma used to bake with whipped cream and straw-berries on top? When Chris gets an A, can we make that for him?"

"Yes," Mr. C says. "I am sure I can find the recipe in Grandma's old book. I will make one for Chris—and I will make one again for you, Karina, when you achieve your goal."

Mr. C leaves, and I help Karina gather her pictures. She keeps the photo of the night sky that I picked on top of the pile. We both stare at it again. "Do you ever wonder if Venus is home to anyone?" she asks.

"I think it's like eight hundred sixty degrees up there," I say.

"Yes," she says. "You would have to be a tardigrade or something to live there."

I can't believe Karina knows about tardigrades too. "Yeah, those creatures can live anywhere—hot or cold. They're so amazing," I say.

And this is amazing too, I think. Karina and I bonding over microscopic animals that can live in extreme conditions. Who knew she'd be fascinated by the weird stuff I like?

I walk home bouncing my basketball, thinking that it's nice to have neighbors you can talk to about everything from sports stars to the actual stars.

It's cool to think about stuff bigger than ourselves.

CHAPTER 9

KARINA

NOW THAT PAPA has found his calling as a math tutor, he is no longer as focused on his to-do list. Papa says he thinks he should have been a math teacher all along, instead of an engineer.

The only problem is that I have to hang around after school on tutorial days. I say I will be fine at home alone, but Papa disagrees. He does not want a discussion.

So I tag along on Tuesdays and Thursdays, do my homework in the cafeteria, and afterward, we take Chris home.

It's funny how it took Papa coming to live with us for Chris's family and mine to become friends. It's hard to remember how we barely used to talk to each other.

Thursday afternoon, Chris, Papa, and I are walking to our car together. It's one of those beautiful autumn days when you want to take a million pictures. The light is warm and golden, and there are a couple trees that are changing colors, which is actually kind of rare in Houston, Texas.

We walk across the empty soccer field and out onto the street that runs alongside it—the street where Papa parks when the parking lot is full.

I tell Papa I'm hungry, and he hands me the bag of strawberries and blueberries he had brought for us to snack on.

I pull out a carton, and Chris, Papa, and I stop in the shade of a large tree and all take handfuls.

"Papa," I say, "when you make Grandma's cake for us, will you make sure to put a ton of strawberries on top?"

"Yum," Chris chimes in. "I'm going to work hard for that cake. And, Karina, that picture you posted yesterday of those geese flying in a V was a winner. I can see it hanging in the gallery now!"

"Thanks!" I tell him. "I'm glad you liked it—and that you both have such faith in me."

I reach for more berries and lick the juice that trickles down my chin.

All these berries must remind Papa of a picture book we used to read together, because he says, "Remember you used to call me your 'Papa Bear'?"

Chris is grinning wide. "Papa Bear? I want to hear."

"Aw, come on, I was just a baby," I say.

"One berry, two berry, pick me a blueberry," Papa recites.

I loved that book. The rhythm of the chant still gets me. Who cares if Chris hears?

"Hatberry, shoeberry, in my canoeberry," I say.

"Under the bridge and over the dam," Papa and I recite together. "Looking for berries, berries for jam."

The innocent rhymes make the berries taste sweeter.

"Mathberry, cakeberry, I cannot wait berry," I say, improvising now.

We are having so much fun that we barely notice the car that crawls by.

When the driver slows down next to us and lowers his window, we expect him to ask for directions, but instead, he pulls the car over ahead of us and gets out.

He surveys the three of us: Chris, Papa, and me.

He walks up to Chris. "You okay?" he asks. Then he reaches over and musses Chris's hair.

It's weird, creepy, the way he touches Chris.

"Sure," Chris says, ducking away. "Why?"

The man spits on the street.

"You know this man?" Papa asks Chris.

"No," Chris replies, and we all keep walking.

Then the man turns to Papa.

"You far from home?" he asks Papa.

"No, sir," Papa says.

I clutch Papa's arm. The bag of berries swings between us.

The man has now dashed ahead of us and is walking backward so he can watch us. He is tall, his eyes are blue, and he smells. And he is prancing on his feet like a fighter throwing punches.

"I think you're *very* far from home, sandman," he says. "Very far."

It's that moment when the man turns into a monster.

He spits again, this time on Papa's shoes.

Despite it being warm out, a chill goes down my spine.

"Hand me the phones," the man barks.

When we don't, he pulls out a knife. He's well within striking distance of Papa.

Everything changes. Everything.

We toss our phones at him, and he hurls them into a bush by the side of the road.

We keep walking, and the man circles us like a vulture homing in on a carcass. His knife glints in the light.

Houses line the street opposite the soccer field, and I see our car at the end of it. But I don't see a soul other than us. I pray that someone will come out with their trash or to walk their dog.

I wonder what the man will do if we make a run for it. Now I reach for Papa's hand and hold it like a lifeline in case the man tries anything.

"You Arab!" he shouts. "Dirty trash! Muslims! Go home!"

I glance at Papa's poker face. Chris is now holding Papa's other hand.

The man comes close to me. "You angry or something, doll?"

"Don't touch her," Papa warns, steel in his voice.

The man shifts his attention to Chris. He is obviously no longer concerned about Chris being safe.

"You a Muslim lover?" he says, and pushes Chris down on the pavement.

"Leave the children alone," Papa says, and steps forward. His tone says he has had enough. But in the face of the threatening knife, there is not much he can do.

"What will you do if I don't, old man?"

In sheer desperation, I throw my backpack at the man, hoping that the knife will fall from his hands. It doesn't.

He growls and then rushes toward Papa.

"Karina, Chris, run!" Papa yells.

Our attacker is not having that. He looks toward me. "You move or try anything else," he says, "and he is dead. You want that?"

I shake my head. Chris and I are rooted to the spot. We wouldn't leave Papa anyway.

Now he shoves Papa hard. As Papa hits the pavement, it feels like a majestic oak has fallen.

The sound of his body hitting the ground makes me sick.

I stifle my gasp as the man kicks Papa.

I don't even recognize the scream that rips out of me.

CHAPTER 10

CHRIS

WHEN THE GUY first approaches us, I think maybe he's someone my parents know. Sometimes I forget random adults. Then he touches my hair in a strange way—and I'm sure I've never seen him before.

When he asks me if I'm okay, I'm confused. Why wouldn't I be okay?

Then I notice his sneer and his darting eyes, and alarm bells ring.

I've played so many video games with bad guys in them, but nothing in my make-believe world has prepared me for this. In the games, I drop-kick monsters, slay them with swords and karate chops—all with the click of a controller. In real life, my self-defense skills are limited to two lessons at the YMCA.

And in those games, the monster *looks* evil. He doesn't wear a plaid shirt and jeans, and drive an ordinary gray Ford Taurus.

My heart feels like it's gonna pound right out of my chest when he calls Mr. Chopra nasty names.

Then he turns on me, pushes me down, and I break my fall with my hands. The burn's intense as the pavement cuts into my skin.

When the monster pushes Mr. C, for a flash I imagine I have the power to cushion his fall and turn the hard ground to soft sand. But I have no power.

I wince as I hear his body smack the ground.

"Terrorists don't belong here," the man says as he gives Mr. C a kick.

I want to leap onto the man's back and pummel him. But he's got that knife, and I'm afraid for us all.

Then I hear the best sound—the rolling of a trash can. The lady pulling it sees us and starts yelling. "Henry! Henry, call nine-one-one!"

The monster retreats. The sound of his boots on the pavement is sharp. Running. Fleeing. Cowardly.

The lady pulls out her phone and takes a picture of his escaping car. Her husband comes out. Says help is on the way.

Karina kneels over her grandfather. "Papa," she says, "an ambulance is coming. You're going to be okay."

But Mr. C doesn't look right. His leg's at a funny angle, and I'll never forget his moans of pain.

I'm praying, *God, please let Mr. C be okay.*

I need to call our parents. I remember that the monster threw our phones into the bushes. I will my legs to move. The bushes are scratchy, but I don't care. I dive in and find the phones. I call my parents and Karina's dad. I barely recognize my own trembling voice.

The ambulance and the police arrive.

They put Mr. C on a stretcher.

As they're loading him into the ambulance, all the parents arrive.

Karina's dad jumps out of the passenger seat, leaving his door wide-open, and races to his father's side. I hear him speaking to Mr. C in Hindi. Then he climbs into the ambulance too.

From that point on, it's all a jumble. A police officer talks to me. So does a paramedic. Mom keeps hugging me and squeezing my arm, and Karina's mom hugs her close too.

An EMT instructs our moms to follow the ambulance to the hospital. Karina's mom looks stunned. The paramedic asks her if she's okay, and Mrs. Chopra sits for a minute and drinks some water.

Karina's gone back to the spot where Mr. C fell. His Gandhi-style glasses are shattered on the street. One of his sandals lies there too. The berries we were eating are strewn all over. The burst strawberries look like splattered blood.

Karina stands there among the wreckage, holding herself tall, and takes pictures. At that moment, I'm so proud to be Karina Chopra's friend.

The police are taking pictures too. Then they pick up Mr. C's glasses and sandal and put them into a plastic bag.

At the hospital, Karina takes pictures of my scraped hands and scratched-up arms, and then we are all separated. I feel every scratch and cut on my arms and my face as they are cleaned and disinfected.

"How come I didn't feel all these scratches when I dove into that bush?" I ask the nurse.

"That was your adrenaline kicking in," he says.

Someone gives Mom a card for a counselor, in case I want to talk to someone about what happened. Then I'm released. I see Mom clutching the card.

Before we go, I ask the doctor, "Are they okay?"

He knows that I mean Karina and Mr. Chopra. "They are," he says. "We'll take good care of them. Don't worry."

At home, Mom and Dad hover over me. Mom sits on my bed and strokes my hair like I'm a little kid again.

Back then, I worried about monsters under my bed, not monsters on a street in my neighborhood.

☆

It's so hard to sleep—every time I close my eyes, I see the monster. I hear his voice.

I remember the way Mr. Chopra's leg looked. I hear him moaning. Will he have to have surgery?

I try to count sheep. But counting makes me think of numbers, and numbers make me think of math, and math reminds of Mr. C.

We laugh a lot, Mr. C and I.

How or why would we find anything funny with math? But we do.

Mr. C uses all kinds of interesting examples when explaining numbers and their relationships. He even figured out a way to use my favorite team—the Rockets—to help me learn. We made a box-and-whisker plot using the height and weight of Rockets players. For real.

So, yeah, we have a good time, Mr. C and I.

I'm so wound up that I decide to call Matt. It's 2:36 a.m., but he's my person. Who else would I call at this hour? The phone rings a bunch of times, and in the quiet of the night, it sounds really loud.

Finally, Matt answers. "Chris?" he says. "What is it?"

I tell him everything, and he listens without breaking in. I'm glad he realizes this is a story that can't be interrupted.

When I'm done, I feel emptied out.

"I wish I was home, Chris," he says.

"Mr. Chopra is a good man," I say.

"I know he is," Matt says.

We are silent.

"This sounds like a hate crime. That man targeted Mr. Chopra because of his race, and because he thought he was Muslim."

"Matt, I couldn't do anything. I couldn't stop him."

I punch my pillow. The unshed tears finally roll down my face.

It's like Matt knows it. He doesn't say a word, but he is there, on the other end of the phone.

At last, I pull myself together. "I don't know how he's doing," I say. "I wish I'd stayed at the hospital. But Mom said there was nothing I could do till tomorrow."

"Mom's right," Matt says.

"Matt, his leg looked awful—"

"Chris, you need to rest," Matt says. "Get some sleep now, okay? You need to be strong for your friends."

He's right, of course. "Good night," I say.

"Love ya," Matt says.

CHAPTER 11

KARINA

MY TEETH CHATTER. It is not that cold in the hospital, but I cannot get them to stop.

Mom bundles me in the warmth of a blanket. Dad makes me drink some hot chocolate from the vending machine.

He holds my hand. "Karina, you're safe."

Are we, though? We thought we were safe a few hours ago, when we were innocently walking to our car, reciting rhymes from an old picture book. I hear the hurtful words that were flung at us. That man is still out there in the world. How can we be safe?

"We don't really know that we are safe anymore, do we?" I say to Dad.

Immediately, I regret saying that, because he looks so miserable. He holds me close, and for a bit I listen to his heart beat.

We don't have much of an update on Papa yet. They

are x-raying his leg. We do know his blood pressure is dangerously elevated.

Time marches on, even if it feels like our lives have been put on pause.

My stomach growls, and we remember we haven't had any dinner. Dad gets us some granola bars, but they taste like ash to me.

Finally, the attending doctor comes in to see us.

The first thing I notice are his blue eyes—like the man who attacked us.

I force myself to look at the doctor. His lips are moving, but I am hardly listening. I take in the rest of him. He is tall and pale, like he has never seen the outside of this hospital. His stethoscope hangs on his wrinkled white coat. His hair is thinning, like Dad's. His touch and tone are so different from the other blue-eyed man.

I must see beyond his eyes, I tell myself. *I must.*

I remind myself that all brown people are not terrorists and that all people with blue eyes are not mean haters.

I try to focus on the present, and I hear him say, "Your daughter is exhausted and in shock. I'm going to give her something to help her sleep. You can take her home, but please don't hesitate to call if you need anything else. We are here to help."

I don't want to leave without seeing Papa, but they

are doing more tests on him and trying to stabilize his blood pressure. The doctor insists that I need to go home and rest.

Dad stays at the hospital, and Mom and I drive home.

On the way home, I worry about Chris. He got pushed to the ground and called names. But he didn't run. He stood by us.

That Chris is all right.

I hope he is okay.

Once we're home, Mom offers food, which I refuse. She gives me one of the pills from the doctor to help me sleep, with a glass of milk.

It is way after midnight when I get into bed, so it's Friday already. I remember that I have a science test on Venn diagrams in six hours. I need to wake up in five hours to make it to school. Then my head hits the pillow, and the world spins away.

I wake up flailing, gasping for air. In my nightmares, I was fighting an enormous dragon-like creature that spat fire, wore a plaid shirt, and yelled, "Go home!"

Before the dream fades, I murmur, "This is my home."

I look at the glowing numbers on the clock and sit up. I can't believe my eyes. It is eight thirty. Mom did not wake me up for school.

"Mom," I call. "Mom."

She hurries in as if she has been waiting for my shout.

"You're awake!" she observes, as if she'd had some doubt that I would ever wake up.

"It's so late," I say. "I missed the bus!"

"It's okay," Mom says. "I thought you should skip school and we could go see Papa."

I nod like that is no big deal, and she fills me in. "Papa has fractured his femur, which is the bone in his thigh—the longest bone in the body. The doctors need to insert a metal rod to help hold the bone in place while it heals. Surgery is scheduled for later today. We're lucky he didn't hurt his head."

"He's going to be fine, right?"

"They think so, honey," Mom replies. "But at his age, recovery is harder and slower. And his blood pressure is still all over the place."

"Yes, but he's going to be fine," I repeat with certainty.

Papa not getting better is not an option.

I get dressed, and Mom and I drive back to the hospital.

"Do you think Chris made it to school?" I ask Mom.

It feels weird to not be going. I've always been proud of my 100 percent attendance record, but after everything that has happened, it suddenly feels unimportant.

"I'll call his mom later," Mom says.

The chilled air and antiseptic smell feel strangely familiar as we enter the hospital building, although before yesterday I had never spent time in a hospital before. It's as if the antiseptic is supposed to mask the smell of disease, infection, and death.

Mom and I tiptoe into the room. Papa snores lightly. An intravenous tube is attached to his right arm, and his hand is blue and bruised where the needle is bandaged down. Papa looks so small and vulnerable that it breaks my heart.

Dad is resting in a chair next to Papa. He has stubble on his face from not shaving.

Papa opens his eyes when he hears us.

"My beta," he says, and reaches his hand out to me. Papa calling me his "daughter" is music to my ears.

I squeeze his free hand. When he winces in pain, I step back, horrified.

Then Papa laughs. Not his usual loud laugh but a paler imitation. Still, it is Papa's laugh.

"I fooled you!" he says.

We exhale. He is trying to help us smile again.

Then he asks about Chris. "Is he okay?"

I nod. "He just got a few scrapes and scratches." I show him the pictures I took of Chris's arms.

"Karina," he says, "God willing, I will be okay. I will come home and we will celebrate. Chris will get an A and your picture will be in the art gallery, and we will have a party."

"Yes," I say. "I like the way you are thinking."

Then, more quietly but with steel in his eyes, Papa says, "Karina, we are not going to let that hater take us down."

I hold back my tears. I nod in agreement.

"That man will not win. He will not defeat us," he says. "I have traveled too far for that."

Dad adjusts Papa's blanket and puts his hand on Papa's shoulder to reassure him.

Papa's words make me feel less scared and alone. This morning, the path was as dark as the night before. It's as if Papa has turned on a flashlight and shown me the way forward. If he is going to fight, so am I.

Papa gives me a look that sees through my soul.

He must notice the small quiver of my lip, because he says, "One berry, two berry, pick me a blueberry."

I swallow the lump in my throat.

"Papa berry, cake berry, get well soon berry," I say.

☆

When the orderlies come to transport Papa to surgery, I hold his hand and walk as far as I am allowed.

I stop before the big swinging doors that read PERSONNEL ONLY.

"See you soon," Papa says.

The clock reads exactly 10:30 a.m. when I walk into the waiting room. Not even twenty-four hours have gone by since an ordinary walk to the car took an unexpected turn and changed our lives.

I scroll through the pictures on my phone. I have lots of images of the smashed berries, the shattered glasses, and the sandal.

I keep going back and forth viewing the pictures. I am not sure what I expect will happen. Will the pictures show me a truth I've missed? It's not like it's a mystery. I know who the victim was. I know who the bad guy was. There are no hidden clues to be found. Yet I keep looking.

Then the pictures tell me what I need to do.

I pick the one of Papa's shattered eyeglasses surrounded by the crushed red fruit. His upturned sandal is also in the frame. At first, I don't know what to say, but then the words write themselves. I start typing.

My grandfather was beaten up and called ugly names yesterday. He was attacked by a stranger who felt that Papa did not belong in America—someone who saw him as a terrorist and a threat. Papa has lived in America longer than he lived in his native India. Today he lies in a hospital bed. My friend Chris and I were with him but couldn't stop the hate. Please pray that Papa recovers. And that soon he will be back to tutoring math and mending broken fences.

I share the post with my friends and family. Papa needs their prayers, and I need their support.

CHAPTER 12

CHRIS

I'M SHOCKED WHEN Mom gives me the option to stay home from school the day after the attack. But I decide to go, thinking Karina might be there.

Before I leave, Mom applies some ointment to my cuts.

"Mom," I say, "will Mr. Chopra get better?"

"Oh, Chris, I pray that he will be fine. What exactly happened, though? How'd it all start?"

As I try to put what happened into words, Mom's eyes get wide. She puts her coffee cup down with shaky hands and asks the question that has been swirling in my head:

"Why would anyone do something like that?"

It's a question neither of us has a good answer for.

☆

School feels weird, and I immediately regret my decision.

68

Karina isn't here after all, and no one knows about what happened to us. A few people ask about my scrapes, but I don't know what to say.

At lunch, I go to the bathroom to sneak a look at my phone. That's when I see that Karina has posted a picture, and I almost drop my phone in the toilet.

The picture is of Mr. Chopra's glasses. The ones he would peer over when I gave him the wrong answer. The glasses that always slid off his nose, that he meant to have tightened.

"Chris," he would say as he polished the smudges off his glasses, "if you focus and leave your fears at the door, math will make sense."

He was right. So I focused—and he helped it all make sense.

I could hear his voice in my head, saying, "Correct, beta!"

Mr. Chopra invited me to his house, and he made me worksheets. He didn't need to do any of that.

He told me stories of when he came to America as a computer science student in 1968. "I was so eager to learn," he said. "I went to university, got a job, and then applied for legal citizenship. It was hard, Chris. So hard. But America has been good to me and given me a life I couldn't have dreamed of."

He doesn't deserve to be disrespected by a man who thinks Mr. C isn't American enough—a guy who thinks he's the more American one. Who made it a contest, anyhow?

I look at the photo again. I notice how Mr. C's broken glasses lie next to a bunch of smashed berries.

Karina Chopra is speaking up. And I see lots of other people have already commented on her post. So I speak up there too. **Hate has no place here,** I write.

In the hallway, I hear people whispering Karina's name, and I see them showing each other Karina's post on their phones.

The word is spreading.

I remember when Matt first started learning to play African drums and he was so excited. He said that a long time ago, people would beat their drums a certain way to send messages to others.

"It was like long-distance communication," he said.

"You mean like phones?" I said.

"Yup," he said, "like phones."

"Way cooler than phones," I said.

"Yup," said Matt, beating his drum.

Social media—that's our drum. Suddenly, I want the world to know what happened to Mr. Chopra. I want the drums to be loud so that everyone will hear our outrage.

☆

"Coach, he's here!" my friend Diego shouts out as I enter the gym for basketball practice.

Coach sees me and says, "Hustle, Daniels!"

We line up to do layups. But I'm off my game. My free throws don't sink, and the ball slides away when I dribble. I don't care, though, because the gym, the game, doesn't feel important today.

Quinn slides up to me, puts his hand on my shoulder, and whispers, "Did you see your girlfriend's picture?"

I shrug his hand off. "I did," I say. "She's my friend, and what happened is terrible."

"She's crying because she spilled her berries," Quinn says.

I shoot a warning look at him, but Quinn has never been one to take a hint.

"Wah! Wah!" he says. "Karina Chopra is complaining because her grandpa broke his glasses."

His voice is like a drill boring a hole in my skull. "Quinn, you don't know anything," I say. "So shut your trap!"

Diego and a new kid named Trevor come over and stand next to me, silently supporting me. I decide I'll show them Karina's picture. I know they'll get it.

"K Chops is whining because someone hated her grandpa's brown behind," Quinn says, laughing.

I step closer to him, curling my hands into fists, and he sneers. "You want to hit me, don't you?"

Now I am in his face. He's right. I want to hit him. He looks scared for a second, and when he turns away, I grab his arm.

"Coach!" he yells. "Chris is looking for a fight."

Coach comes running. "What's going on?"

Quinn says, "He started it."

"Chris Daniels," Coach says, looking puzzled, "I didn't expect this from you."

"It's not Chris's fault," Diego tells him.

By this time, lots of kids have circled around us.

Coach is holding Quinn and me apart. "Did you start this?" he asks me.

I stare at my shoes and don't answer.

Coach shakes his head, confused. "Okay then. Chris, you'll have to sit out today. Starting a fight also means detention, my friend."

Quinn laughs.

I sit on the sidelines and fume.

I should've punched him. What's wrong with Quinn, anyway? And why are there so many haters?

CHAPTER 13

KARINA

PAPA HAS BEEN in surgery for a while, and each minute feels like an hour. I keep remembering how the doctor warned Dad that surgery at Papa's age can have complications.

I glance at the waiting-room clock. It's 1:00 p.m. On a typical Friday, I would be in sixth period.

Dad paces. Mom knits and dozes in a chair. We all worry and pray.

Nobody is voicing the thing that scares us the most: Will Papa walk again?

Will he be able to climb stairs? How will he get to his room if he can't? He is always on the move—cooking, fixing, and doing.

Papa would absolutely hate being dependent.

To pass time, I begin taking pictures of the waiting room, the nurses' station, and the doctors rushing around. Anything to take my mind off the fact that Papa is on an operating table with his leg cut open.

"Karina," Dad says, "was there anything at all you can think of that might have set the man off yesterday?"

Mom puts down her knitting and looks at me, hoping I will say more. I already told her we did nothing. *Just being us on the street set this man off*, I want to say.

But the words get stuck in my throat as I look around the waiting room that the staff has tried to make look more like a living room than a hospital. There are couches, colorful cushions, even a few throws. There are plants strategically placed around the room. I notice that none of them are dying and award brownie points to the hospital.

I also notice that there are lots of tissue boxes scattered around the room, breaking the illusion. Reminding us that this is also a place for upset, sometimes grieving families.

I stare at the weave on the throw blankets. They are red and blue, and they remind me of the spilled berries. I keep staring. I want to tell my parents what happened, but how?

I look down at my phone and go to my pictures. I've always been more comfortable saying things with my photographs. This is why I took them. I knew there might be times I would not be able to find words—times I would need the images to share my experiences. With my pictures, I can remember all the details.

My parents stare at the pictures of the attack scene

on the screen. I wonder if I should mention that I posted the one of Papa's broken glasses, but then I brush away the thought. How does it matter?

Then I begin to tell them everything I can remember.

Even as I narrate the events, I wonder if there *was* anything I could have done differently.

"We were walking along, minding our own business," I say. "The man got out of his car and attacked us just because he didn't like how we looked."

I pause for a moment and then ask, "Did that man forget that his grandparents or great-grandparents were probably immigrants too?"

The line on Dad's forehead is deep. Mom takes tissues from a box.

"Karina," Dad says, "I am so sorry."

I see a tear roll down Dad's face. I have never seen him cry before, and I break down too.

Mom puts her arms around us both. Hugging us to comfort and reassure us.

"If only I had never suggested that Papa be a tutor," she says.

Surely, she can't blame herself.

"Trisha, stop. You know that had nothing to do with it," Dad says. "Tutoring makes Papa happy. He feels needed and useful."

"Yes," I say, agreeing with Dad. "Papa was so happy yesterday. We all were."

I get us another box of tissues, and between the three of us, we use almost the whole box.

Then we continue to wait for someone to come update us on the surgery.

Finally, the surgeon appears. Dad jumps to his feet. I hold my breath. "Your father is resting. The surgery went well. We'll know more after a day or so."

My parents and I hug at this good news. It is a step in the right direction, but I am still troubled. More than anything, I want to know that Papa is going to get better and walk again. Until the stars align and that happens, this galaxy won't feel like home.

CHAPTER 14

CHRIS

ON SATURDAY MORNING, I tell my parents I want to visit Mr. C at the hospital.

Both my parents are surprised. My hatred of hospitals is well-known. When I was eight, I fell off my skateboard and busted up my lip. The metallic taste of my own blood freaked me out—but worse was when I got stitches and felt like I was gonna pass out. Since then, hospitals have been on my Places I'd Rather Not Revisit list.

Dad slaps me on the back. "My boy's growing up," he says. "A little blood doesn't scare him anymore."

"Dad, this is serious," I say.

He looks at me for a minute and surprises me by saying, "Of course it is. I didn't mean to joke. I'm happy you're standing by your friends."

Mom takes the banana bread she made for the Chopras out of the oven and says she will drive me.

☆

At the hospital, we find Karina's mom in the waiting area. I leave the moms there and go to see Mr. C.

I walk through the hushed corridors toward room 2154. I hate the smell of hospitals, but for Mr. C, I will deal. A man with an IV pole and a flapping hospital gown walks in front of me. I try not to look at his butt. Can you squeeze past a sick man? I decide not to.

At the door to Mr. C's room, I pause. Karina's sitting by her grandfather's bed. She is reading Roald Dahl's *The BFG* aloud, with different voices and all.

It's so Karina that I smile.

Mr. C notices me hovering by the door. "Chris," he says. "Chris, come on in!"

I enter the room and see that Mr. C is hooked up to an IV and that his thigh is bandaged. I try not to stare.

"Come here, beta. Come here," he says.

Hearing him call me "beta" is the best, and I relax a little. I inch closer and stand right by his bed.

Of course Mr. C wants to check out *my* arm and look at *my* scratches before I have a chance to ask him how he is.

There's a knock on the door, and two police officers enter the room.

I've been around more police officers in the last forty-eight hours than ever before in my life.

Their uniforms are starched. They have guns in their holsters.

"I'm Sergeant Muniz with the Special Crimes Unit," the older one says, "and this is Detective Willis." They both shake Mr. C's hand.

The men say they are investigating the incident. They want to ask Mr. C a few questions and have him look at a few photographs to identify the perpetrator. They suggest that Karina and I wait outside.

"They should stay," Mr. C says. "They were both with me when I was attacked."

"Aha," Sergeant Muniz says. "I didn't realize that these were the children. You must be Karina and Chris."

I stand as straight as I can when they shake hands with me, and try to make sure my grip is firm.

"I'm sorry that y'all had this terrible experience," the sergeant says after Mr. C tells him all that he remembers from the attack.

Then he goes to ask our mothers' permission for Karina and me to identify the attacker too.

The sergeant explains that he will show me the pictures first, then Karina. Detective Willis takes the pictures from a manila envelope.

The picture of that man stares at me. He's leaning against the same car he was driving that day. He isn't smiling or anything—his lips are zipped shut, like they should have been that day instead of spewing garbage.

On TV dramas, this kind of stuff looks exciting; maybe it's the soundtrack. But in real life, it's super scary.

It takes me the blink of an eye to identify the man.

When it's Karina's turn, she agrees.

"You all identified the same man," the detective tells us.

"Yes," Mr. Chopra says. "We could never forget that face."

Karina holds his hand.

"You'll find him, right?" I say. "And put him in jail?"

"We'll do our best, Chris," the detective says. He puts the pictures back in the envelope. Like putting the ogre in a manila cage.

"We tracked the license plates of his car. The lady who had her husband call nine-one-one, Anne Maxwell, got a picture of his plate as he was driving away," the sergeant says.

"I remember her doing that," Karina says. "Thankfully!"

"Do you know anything about him?" Mr. C asks.

"Other than that he's a monster," I say.

The sergeant looks at me. "Yes. He's had minor offenses in the past, and lately has shown up on our radar. He's been involved with some nationalist groups that are anti-immigrant and anti-minority. We keep an eye on them."

"I have lived in this country for fifty years," Mr. C says, "and I have never been treated like this."

"We're so sorry this happened," Detective Willis says.

"Thank you for all you are doing!" Mr. C says. He shakes hands with the police officers again.

After they are gone, he looks exhausted.

The world's making me feel sad and helpless. I worry about Mr. C and hope his pride wasn't crushed too badly that horrible day, in front of us. I want to make sure he is treated right, with the respect he deserves.

☆

At home, Mom and I find Dad reading the *Spring Hill News*.

When we tell him that the police found the guy who attacked Mr. C, he holds out the newspaper to us. There's a small article on the attack.

Mr. Shiv Chopra, a new resident of Spring Hill, was attacked by an unidentified assailant who fled the scene, on Thursday near Spring Hill Middle School. Mr. Chopra, who was accompanied by his granddaughter and her friend, was pushed to the ground and kicked. The attack is being investigated as a suspected hate crime. Mr. Chopra was admitted to Methodist Hospital in Houston. If anyone has any information, please contact the police.

I can confirm it was a hate crime—they don't need to investigate that.

"This article tells some basic facts, but it still misses so much," I say to Mom and Dad. "Like what about all the hateful things he said to Mr. C and Karina and me? And what about all the pain he's putting such a good man through?"

Mom and Dad exchange a look. "Chris," Mom says, "we couldn't agree more."

"He called Mr. Chopra a Muslim," I say, "but Karina's family isn't even Muslim."

"And this is America, where you're supposed to be free to practice any religion or be an atheist," says Mom. "It shouldn't matter."

"That man knew nothing about Mr. C—or the Chopras," says Dad. "But I have to admit, I didn't either, till Mr. Chopra started to tutor you."

"True," I say. "I'm so glad we *did* get to know him. Otherwise, we would have never found out what a cool guy he is."

As we talk, my mind spins. A few days ago I'd have never imagined discussing hate crimes with my parents. But here we are, in our kitchen, talking about heavy stuff instead of what we'll grill for dinner. I wish the circumstances that brought us to this were different, but I'm glad we're having the conversation.

Like Mr. C says, you have to be able to imagine a better world to make it a reality.

CHAPTER 15

KARINA

A FEW HOURS after Chris leaves, Papa goes to sleep and my parents and I drive home. It feels good to be home after the long day in the hospital. Mom and Dad are watching what sounds like a Hindi movie down in the living room. Then there is a pause in the Bollywood tune.

When I hear them talking, I head to my spot at the top of the stairs where I can listen in.

"Jay," Mom is saying, "I have received thirty-two phone calls since this morning."

"It's the weekend," Dad says. "Everyone is wanting to know what happened, and they finally have the time to call."

I lean against the wall.

I hear Mom mention that a lot of the family has seen the pictures I posted and that they are worried and want to know what's happening. She hasn't had time to check social media, never mind answer her constantly ringing phone, with all that is going on.

"Don't worry about the family," Dad says. "I will get in touch with them. They will be happy to hear the surgery went well and that Papa is recovering."

"Okay. But do it soon, please," Mom says. "Rumors are spreading. Your cousin Sarla from Chicago heard from another relative that Papa was dying."

"Wow!" Dad says. "That's a leap."

"Well, you know how rumors spread," Mom says. "It took me a while to calm her down."

Hearing this reminds me of a game we used to play when I was little called Telephone. It was funny the way the words changed as they were relayed from one person to another. The more distorted the message got from the original, the more we would laugh. This is probably what is happening now, based on my postings. Except now, it's not funny.

Apparently, my first post—of the smashed glasses—left relatives unsure of how badly Papa was hurt. Some thought he was mugged. And people wondered, since I was with him, if I was okay.

My second post, from the hospital, was of the swinging doors with the PERSONNEL ONLY sign, and the hashtag #Surgery. That got lots more relatives calling to find out the details.

Dad says to Mom, "Why didn't you tell Karina not

to share this? We would have told people once Papa was better."

"You think I monitor every picture that Karina posts?" Mom snaps. "That child takes a million pictures of everything. You were in the hospital too when she was photographing things. Why didn't you stop her?"

I cannot believe it. Now they are fighting about me.

"That last one was right as my father was being taken into surgery," Dad says. "I wasn't worrying about Karina posting pictures at that moment."

"Neither was I," says Mom. "Jay, what if it gets beyond friends and family? What if this becomes truly public? Could this attract more haters?"

"I can't think about that right now, Trisha," Dad says.

Finally, they are both quiet.

I get up and go join my parents. I can't have them blaming each other for my actions.

Mom strokes my hair when I sit by her. "Karina, I didn't know you had been sharing pictures. We have gotten a lot of calls."

"I should have told you when I showed you the picture of Papa's glasses that I had posted it. I'm sorry I didn't," I say. "But I have gotten a lot of support from people who have seen the pictures. It reminds me that most people *don't* hate. That has helped me get through the last few days."

My parents seem to understand.

"Okay," Mom tells me. "Don't worry—we will deal with the relatives."

"But let's not mention this to Papa right now," Dad says. "When I was growing up, he always told us to keep our head down and work, and not share our business."

"My dad used to say that too," Mom says. "Our parents accepted the little slights as the price that they had to pay for being new in the country. But maybe things are different now. Karina's generation wants and demands more."

Yes, things are different, I want to say.

Also, I am not new. I was born here.

It is my country.

CHAPTER 16

CHRIS

ON SUNDAY AFTER church, I sit at my desk and stare at my math homework till the words and numbers start to swim and my eyes cross. I get frustrated and throw my eraser across the room—which is pretty dumb because I need it a few minutes later to erase what I've done and start again.

But I make no progress, so I head outside to shoot some hoops.

I dribble the ball from the end of the driveway toward the basket on the garage door. I have my arm raised, ready to shoot, when I am interrupted by "Chris!"

It's Karina.

I stop what I'm doing to talk to her. "How's your grandfather?" I ask.

"Much better than when you saw him yesterday," Karina says. "The doctors want to make him stand tomorrow. They say it is super important to do that."

"Oh yeah?" I say. "Will he have a cast and crutches?"

"No cast. He might need crutches or a walker, or even a wheelchair for a bit. I don't know," she says. "I want to be there for him, but my parents say I have to go back to school tomorrow."

I can see she's anxious. Her forehead is all scrunched up.

"It'll be okay," I say.

"Will it?" Karina asks. "School is going to be weird with everyone knowing what happened. So many kids have commented and shared my pictures—kids I've barely ever even talked to."

"I don't think it's weird," I tell her. "People are upset. And a lot of them want to support you."

I don't share the rude stuff Quinn said to me in the gym on Friday. She doesn't need to know.

We both kind of stand there.

"Karina, it'll be okay," I say again, but of course I don't really know. What I really want to say is, *Karina, you shouldn't care who knows, because you're in the right.* Plus, *We're in this together.* But I don't say any of this aloud, since I worry it'll sound as cheesy as a plate of nachos.

Karina asks, "Did you do your math worksheet?"

"I started it," I say. "But how do you even know about that worksheet? You weren't in school Friday."

"Ashley came by and brought me my homework."

"So you know how to do those problems?" I ask.

"Yeah, I do. Papa and I are ahead of the class."

"Ah!" I say. "Of course you are."

Then it occurs to me—that "ah" has triggered an aha moment—if Mr. Chopra has already taught Karina the stuff we're now learning in class, then she could teach me. It would be like passing the knowledge from Mr. C to me, only through Karina.

But first, I need to find the words to ask her.

"Good luck," she says. "I'll see you tomorrow."

I nod, and she walks away.

She's at the end of the driveway when I scream, "Karina!"

"Yes?" she says, looking startled by my desperate-sounding yell.

You're pathetic, Daniels, I tell myself. *Mr. C is in the hospital fighting to walk with a metal rod in his leg, and you just need to find the courage to ask Karina Chopra for help.*

"Karina, do you think you could teach me math?" I make myself say. "Like be my tutor, till your grandfather recovers? Those darn worksheets are killing me!"

She smiles. "You look pretty healthy to me. But sure. I have some time now before we go back to the hospital. Is now good?"

"Yes!" I tell her. "My place?"

"Sure," she says. "But, Chris, let's make a deal. If I help you with math, could you teach me how to shoot a basket?"

"You got it!" I say. "You can call me Coach Chris, but we'll have to tackle math first."

"Cool. I'll be back with my notes."

Karina has never been inside my house. I race around, clear the dining room table of junk mail, and set out my books and papers. Then I make popcorn, because what if she's hungry and wants a snack?

She eyes the bowl when she comes over. "How did you know I love popcorn?" she says. "My fave, though, is caramel popcorn. Papa loves cheddar popcorn."

"Filing that kernel away," I say.

"So you can pop it out when you need it?" she asks without missing a beat.

Yaas! Karina likes puns as much as me. It's weird how she lives next door and there's still so much we don't know about each other.

We get down to work, and Karina is just like her grandfather; she wastes no time.

"The equation," she says, "is a question in numbers."

"It is?" I scratch my head.

"If you wanted to read a book that had a hundred pages in five days, how many pages would you read per day?" she asks, all teacher-like.

"Twenty," I say.

"You solved it," she says, writing it out in equation format.

Then she goes on to break it down, explaining order of operations and what an x variable is.

Before I know it, it's been more than an hour. The worksheet is done, and we are eating popcorn.

"Chris," she says. "That man . . . You know, the man who attacked us . . ."

"Yeah," I say. "I call him 'the monster.'"

"I do too," she tells me. "The monster in the plaid shirt. It makes me scared that he is still out there on the streets."

"Me too," I say. "It's horrible that he could just do what he did and get away."

"Chris, do you think there are others who think and hate like that?"

"You know there are."

"I feel so helpless and scared," Karina confesses. "And then I feel really, really angry. I want to punch something other than my pillow."

"My pillow's been getting a workout too," I tell her. Karina is the only person I know, other than Papa, who knows how this feels.

My parents, her parents, our friends, the police officers—they all care for us, but only we know the pit-in-the-stomach fear.

After I visited Mr. C in the hospital yesterday and

we identified the hater, I went for a bike ride because I couldn't stand Mom fussing over me. But even on the bike trail, I couldn't lose the image of that man. I was constantly looking over my shoulder.

Karina reaches for the last of the popcorn. "Papa says the haters will not win."

"He's right!" I say. Under my breath, I sing, "Let it go . . . let it go . . ."

Karina grins. "Really, Chris? *Frozen*?"

"I'm allowed."

Karina joins in—and even though we both know we can't just let it go, it feels good to sing together.

CHAPTER 17

KARINA

PAPA'S HOSPITAL ROOM feels like a party on Sunday evening. So many of our friends from the Indian community have gathered to visit and help. They make plans to take shifts at the hospital during the week so Mom and Dad can still manage their store.

When I refer to my dad's friends as Dev Uncle and Sri Uncle and Ravi Uncle, the nurses are confused. "How many siblings does your dad have?" one of them asks.

I explain to them that even though I call people "uncle" or "aunty," they are not Dad's actual siblings. "We Indians call our family friends 'uncle' and 'aunty' as if they are blood relatives," I say.

Papa is amused by all this. And I know he is really feeling better when he complains about the hospital food. He even teases a nurse, asking her to bring him a paratha stuffed with gobi, with dahi on the side.

"What?" asks the nurse.

"It's a flatbread," I say. "Stuffed with spiced cauliflower, with a yogurt dipping sauce on the side. That's what he wants."

"Sounds yummy," she says, giving him his pill. "Save some for me when you do get it."

Mrs. Kumar, one of our family friends, promises that she will bring some for everyone, and we cheer.

We are all feeling giddy because we are so relieved that Papa seems like his old self. He looks like his old self too, having shaved in honor of his visitors.

But while smiles dominate in his room, in the hallways and waiting areas, it's different.

☆

I hear snippets of conversation:

"How could something like this happen?"

"The man called him a terrorist for no reason—just because of how he looked!"

"No one should be treated like that! What's going on in this country?"

"Is it safe anywhere anymore?"

"Thank God the children weren't hurt."

"There is no escaping our new reality."

Finally, the visitors leave. Dad and I remain while Papa rests, exhausted from all the company.

The room is silent except for a hum and occasional

beeps. I no longer jump every time a machine hiccups. I turn the pages of my book quietly.

When the police officers we met yesterday show up, Papa opens his eyes and sits up.

"Mr. Chopra," Sergeant Muniz says. "Good to see you looking better."

"We have an update on the perpetrator," Detective Willis says. "Thanks to Anne Maxwell, who helped y'all on the day of the attack."

I don't think the word *perpetrator* sounds evil enough. I prefer our word: *monster*.

Detective Willis fills us in. "Police spotted the car about two hundred miles from here, between Austin and Dallas. The driver tried to make a run for it and led the police on a chase."

"What happened?" I blurt out. "Did they catch him?"

"Well," Detective Willis says, "yes and no. He drove straight into a tree, and his car exploded into flames."

Dad sucks in his breath.

"They had to identify him from his dental records," the detective says.

The monster is dead. The world seems to stop spinning for a moment.

The officers are talking to Dad and Papa, but their voices are far away. All I hear is, *The monster is dead.* He is no longer walking around hating on others.

I move from my chair to sit next to Papa on his bed and hold his hand.

We both breathe a sigh of relief.

After the officers leave, I call Chris and tell him the news. He is quiet, but he doesn't have to say a thing, because after a few moments of silence, I hear him exhale too.

CHAPTER 18

CHRIS

AS WE BOARD the bus on Monday morning, Karina points to her blue T-shirt. "My lucky shirt. I need it for my first day back."

I smile and point to my striped socks. "My lucky socks. I need them for the math test."

"Daniels," Quinn pipes up, "you slumming with the nerds?"

"Nope, Quinn," I say. "I'm hanging with my friends."

I plonk my backpack next to Diego and Trevor instead of Quinn and his posse. I am changing teams, and I like it.

The monster who attacked us is gone, but there are still plenty of Quinns in the world.

☆

When we arrive at school, Ashley tells Karina and me we are going to take a quick detour before going inside.

"Diego, Trevor, and I have a surprise for you guys. Come see what we did."

They lead us across the soccer field to the tree near the sidewalk at the edge of the school grounds. The spot where it all happened.

A big green heart has been chalked on the street around the berry stains.

"It's just like the leaf hearts you drew on my valentine," Karina says as she hugs Ashley.

Then she reads the sign pinned to the tree—also in the shape of a green heart: "Spread Love, Not Hate."

A few others have copied Ashley's heart and hung their hearts on the tree. They flutter in the breeze.

What they've done for us is so cool—it makes me feel that with all of them on my team, I've got the best lineup.

Then Karina does her thing. She takes pictures. *Click. Click. Click.*

We head back to the school building. Before we go our separate ways, I tell Karina I hope her lucky shirt does the trick for her. And then I add, in my deepest voice, "May the Force be with you!"

She cracks up. "May the equations work for you!"

☆

When I walk into the gym, Coach is watching me like a

hawk. *Maybe he's worried about another fight*, I think. But instead, he comes up to me and says, "How you doing, Chris?"

"Okay," I say. "Why?"

"Ms. Trotter told me what happened," he says.

Coach is a man of few words, but I know what stuff he's talking about.

"Karina's grandfather is in the hospital," I say. "With a bad broken leg."

"What's happening to this world?" Coach says, shaking his head.

During gym class, we begin our game, and Quinn refuses to pass the ball to me. Even when it's clear I can probably make a shot and I yell, "Quinn, here," he doesn't listen.

We are behind in the first quarter.

There's also a moment when I am right under the basket, unguarded. It's like a gift from God. "Pass the ball!" I yell.

Thump. Thump. Nope. Nope.

He passes it to his friend Alex. Alex holds on to the ball and dribbles it across the court. *Thump. Thump. Thump.*

It's as if they can't hear or see me. Alex doesn't make it. Coach whistles time and gives me a look that says, *Hang in there.* I take a deep breath.

The next time Quinn runs to the basket, he passes to

Alex and then, out of nowhere, Diego comes charging in like a galloping horse, steals the ball, and passes it to me. I am so stunned, I almost don't catch it.

I hear Trevor yelling for me to shoot, and I do. I score!

In the locker room, I keep out of Quinn's way, but he finds me. "You think you're pretty great," he says, "but you're really not."

Diego comes over. "Chris," he says, "let's go."

Quinn elbows Diego against the locker as we walk out.

At lunch, Diego, Trevor, and I join Karina, Ashley, and a few others.

I notice kids whispering and giving Karina and our table side glances. I know she sees them too. She knows most of them are supportive, but she is adjusting to the attention. I watch her take a deep breath, then lift her burrito.

"Why can't you trust a burrito?" I say to lighten the mood.

"Why?" she says, playing along.

"Because they spill their beans."

Karina laughs. "What kind of music does the burrito like?" she says.

"Wrap, of course!" I say.

Success!

After lunch, the corridor is packed with kids all trying to get to their classes. Karina, Ashley, and I are like salmon swimming upstream. And we can't help hearing the murmurs of a bunch of eighth graders in front of us . . .

"That picture she posted was intense."

"Is she the pretty Indian girl?"

"Did you see all the notes and stuff on the tree?"

"Jennifer's little sister is her friend."

"Her grandfather is in the hospital."

"Why did they attack him?"

"They thought he was like a foreigner, a terrorist."

"He's not, though," Karina says in a loud, clear voice. "A foreigner."

Her words ring out, stopping everyone in their tracks. Kids turn to look at her.

"My grandfather has lived in this country for fifty years. He is a citizen. A good one. *Not* a terrorist."

Nobody knows what to say at first.

A few kids say they are sorry for what happened.

Then the bell rings, and everybody runs off.

Karina hugs herself, as if she doesn't believe that she said something aloud.

"Chris, should I have kept my mouth zipped?"

"No way!" I tell her. "What you said was great. It was so cool you spoke up!"

But Karina doesn't seem convinced. I notice she spends most of social studies staring into space. At the end of class, Ms. Trotter gives her a card and a hug.

On the bus ride home, I ask her about the card.

"Ms. Trotter said to open it later," she says.

Ashley nudges Karina and smiles. "Now is later already."

"Maybe she gave you a gift card for ice cream? And you want to treat us?" I say hopefully.

Karina pulls the card out of her backpack and tears the envelope open.

The card has a globe on it, circled with red hearts. She glances at it and then reads it aloud.

Dear Karina,

> *You may not know who G. K. Chesterton was, but he said, "We are all in the same boat upon a stormy sea, and we owe each other a terrible loyalty."*

> *I am here for you,*
> *Amelia Trotter*

Karina hugs the card.

We are all quiet for a moment. Absorbing the words.

"Did you know her name was Amelia?" asks Ashley.

"A-me-lia. It's perfectly right for her," says Karina. She and Ashley both have goofy grins on their faces.

"The Chesterton dude is all right too," I say.

"He is on point," says Karina. "We are all in this together."

"That's the truth," Ashley says.

When we get off the bus, Karina says, "Chris, if I ever get a gift card for ice cream, I will totally share it with you."

"Can we get sprinkles too?" I ask.

"For sure," Karina says, "because life is better with sprinkles."

CHAPTER 19

KARINA

THE PHYSICAL THERAPIST and a nurse are in Papa's room when we get there after school on Monday. The physical therapist is a slim woman with biceps that ripple, and the nurse is a huge man with a sweet smile.

While they talk, I check out the giant card someone left for Papa. It looks so cheerful that a stranger might think that Papa just slipped and fell, rather than the more brutal truth. It is full of hearts and signatures and get-well-soon messages. Some are even written in Hindi.

I take a picture of the card and post it with a bunch of hashtags—#SurgerySuccessful, #HatersWontWin, #Stay-Strong, #OneStepAtATime, and #SupportHeals.

Now as the physical therapist helps Papa up, she says, "You can do this, Mr. Chopra. You have fans out there."

"Yes, yes, I can," Papa says.

Papa grunts as they hoist him up. The nurse and the physical therapist hover on either side. Papa takes a step and then another.

I watched Papa wince in pain as they made him stand for the first time after his surgery. I can only imagine how hard this must be. Papa has to regain his muscle strength and learn to bear weight on his injured leg. Each day, he will take a few more steps.

I think back to when we were upset because Papa was reorganizing our house and could not sit still. I remember Mom with her coloring book and Dad stressing over the Daniels's fence, and I thought the world was ending because I couldn't find computer paper. I miss those problems.

After a walk around the room, Papa is helped back into his bed. The physical therapist and nurse joke with him and cheer him on before they leave.

Papa's forehead glistens with sweat. I sit on his bed and hold his hand while he closes his eyes for a bit.

This is the hard part of the day. But I have noticed that Papa's face lights up when he has visitors. He speaks in Punjabi, Hindi, and Hinglish, and laughs and laughs. For a few hours, he forgets the needles and the blood pressure gauges, and the long, uncertain road to walking again.

I would do anything for my grandfather, and as I sit close to him, I decide that when he comes home, we are going to give him the best party ever. The doctors have said that if all continues to go well, Papa could be discharged from the hospital later this week and then go to a rehab facility for a few weeks. That will give me plenty of time to try to figure out the recipe for Grandma's famous strawberry cake.

☆

When Papa has some energy back, he sits up and points to the album I placed beside his bed. "I am so happy you found my album," he tells me.

"Mom thought it would cheer you up, and I wanted to see if you were always this handsome," I tell him, eager to look through the old pictures.

Opening the album is like finding a video of laughing babies on the internet. Then you want to watch the next one, and the one after. I keep turning pages.

"Why haven't you shown this to me before?" I exclaim when I see pictures of him as a boy with his grandparents. His grandfather looks just like him, and his mother and sisters wear flowers in their long braids, and silky saris.

"I am happy you are seeing it now," he says. "You should know our family's stories."

Papa points to a picture of him and Grandma in front of a blue single-story house. "Once upon a time, we lived here."

They look so young and so proud of being first-time homeowners in their adopted country.

"See, we planted marigolds in the garden to remind us of India."

I lift the album and take a closer look at my grandparents' dream home.

"In that house, we had an oven," he says. "It was yellow. That is when Grandma learned to bake. Back then, not even the richest man in our small village in Punjab owned an oven. Oh, we felt rich, your grandma and I."

Then he turns the page, and there is Grandma wearing pants and a shirt with big flowers on it, carrying a matching purse.

"Your grandma learned enough English to get a job as a teller, in a bank near our house. Her English may not have been the best, but she could account for every penny, at home and at work." The pride in his voice is unmistakable.

These stories of their early life make me wonder about it more, and I say, "What did it feel like to leave everything behind?"

"I missed my family—my mother worrying if I had eaten enough, squabbling with my sisters over card games. And we missed having people around who had known us since birth. We even missed the man in the market who made barfi, the sweet milk dessert that you love, and the woman who haggled over the price of okra and tomatoes. And we missed the smells of the market, the air after the rain . . ."

Papa is quiet for a minute and looks as if he is far away.

Then he says, "We used to live for those visits back home. But then ita Aunty was born, your father was born, and *this* became home. With each visit to India, we felt more like visitors."

I'm not sure I understand all he is saying, but I file the words away so I can figure them out later.

We keep looking at more pictures till the question bursts out into the open: "Papa," I say, "are you angry?"

Anger has overcome *me* so many times over the last few days, coming in waves that feel like they will knock me off my feet.

"I am glad that your grandmother isn't around to see this day," he tells me.

"What are we going to do, Papa?" I ask.

"For years, I thought that maybe people did not know any better when they made fun of our accents, because for the most part, America welcomed me and my family. But now I understand there are just some people who do not want people like us here. Karina, maybe we have to give back now by fighting for the America we believe in."

I nod as Dad appears with coffee. Papa and I get silent.

"Did I miss something?" Dad asks.

Papa shakes his head.

Dad picks up the photo album. "I have not seen these pictures in decades," he says, and flips it open, adding details to the stories Papa had told, pointing to his first bike lying on the lawn in one of the pictures, and telling me how he and his sister first baked chicken nuggets in that same yellow oven.

As we are leaving, Papa says, "Karina, I know you have been busy, but have you decided which of your pictures you will enter for that competition?"

"No, I haven't had time," I say, and the truth of that surprises me.

"Well, *do not* forget about it," Papa tells me. "We are going to celebrate when you get in the show. And that reminds me, I left some math worksheets in the kitchen for Chris, and for you too. Please get them. I want you both to practice."

At home, I find the folder marked "Math" exactly where Papa said I would find it. It has separate worksheets for me and for Chris. And at the bottom of the stack is the cake recipe.

My heart surges with love for my organized Papa. He was going to make the cake for Chris when he got the A and for me when I got in the art gallery show. Papa had the recipe in there, ready to go for us. Now we will make it for him instead.

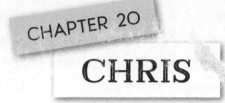

CHAPTER 20

CHRIS

TYPICALLY ON FRIDAY, we order pizza for dinner. A Daniels family tradition. On Saturday, there's usually a basketball game, and on Sunday, we go out to eat after church and then I do homework.

But last Thursday, Mr. Chopra was attacked and I was called a "Muslim lover." On Friday, he had surgery and I worried all day. On Saturday, I visited him in the hospital and identified a criminal, and on Sunday, I was told that a man had died and it made me relieved.

Is this really my life?

I'm glad I'm not the only one who thinks everything is out of whack in the world. On Tuesday afternoon, I can't believe what I see when I pass the memorial Ashley, Trevor, and Diego made for Mr. C.

Everything has multiplied. There are lots more flowers and cards, and a couple of balloons. People have also hung a bunch more of the green hearts with notes showing support. Someone has placed a picture of Karina and her grandfather on the tree too. It's almost as if the flowers and hearts are pushing away the hate.

It makes me feel so much better to see this. It's like everyone in school knows what happened now. They've seen Karina's pictures, and they have her back.

When I see a familiar-looking woman walking toward me, I try to remember how I know her.

Then it clicks.

Duh, I tell myself. *It's the lady who saved you when she rolled out her trash can.* If it wasn't for her taking the picture of the monster's fleeing car, he might not have been caught.

"Chris?" she calls out in a voice that's so different from the panicky one she used that day.

She reaches out a hand to shake mine. "I'm Anne Maxwell."

She's carrying a small bunch of flowers and points to the memorial. "I was so happy to see this."

She asks about Karina and Mr. Chopra, and I fill her in.

"I want to help in any way I can," she tells me.

When she hands me her card, I see that she works for the *Lonestar Times*.

Mrs. Maxwell takes some pictures of the memorial. "I'd like to put a picture of this in the paper and post it online. It's such a hopeful sign for our community. I want people to see that love can fight hate."

"Karina has been sharing pictures online too," I say. "I'm sure she'd like you to follow her."

"Has she? I'd love to see them," she says, and I share Karina's handle.

"Thanks!" Mrs. Maxwell says as she walks away. "I'll see you soon, I hope."

I'm about to ride off on my bike when I spy a menu from an Indian restaurant next to one of the cards. I recognize the logo of the restaurant. Bombay Palace. What's that doing there?

I prop my bike and pick it up.

Curry stinks is written across the front in black marker. Undeniable. Indelible.

I remember that note that was passed to Karina last year, and it's a pretty easy guess who might've put that menu among the flowers.

I tear the menu to bits.

CHAPTER 21

KARINA

TODAY IS THE day Papa gets discharged. A nurse pushes him in a wheelchair to the hospital foyer. My arms are full of flowers and a bouquet of get-well-soon balloons.

"I wish I was going home," Papa says. "But I need the rehab."

"Papa," I say. "Two weeks will fly by—you'll be home before Halloween."

It turns out the rehab center is much nicer than the hospital. We settle Papa in his room. Dad steps out to take care of insurance business, and I arrange Papa's family photos and his Krishna idol on his bedside table.

Papa says, "Karina, Rita Aunty called me this morning. She said you had put a picture from that day on the internet?"

He sounds surprised that I would do that. I guess I am surprised that he didn't hear till now.

"Can I see it?" he asks.

I hand him my phone, and he takes his time looking

at the picture, reading my caption and other people's comments.

When he hands my phone back, he says, "Beta, does the world need to know our pain?"

I don't say anything.

"We were raised to keep family matters within the family," he says.

I don't know how to respond to that. I guess there is some truth to what Papa believes, but sometimes sharing a burden makes it easier to bear.

"We are immigrants," he says. "We have to be careful."

"Yes, almost everybody is or was an immigrant in this country, Papa," I say.

"Not the way we are," he says forcefully.

"You remember when you said we can't let hate win?" I ask.

"Yes, I do."

"Well, Papa," I say, "sharing my photos is my way of speaking up. Of fighting hate."

Papa nods at me, and I think he gets it.

Then he scrunches his forehead and says, "I am trying to understand this posting thing. So each person can share with their friends?"

I nod. "Yes, if they want."

"And then *they* share too. So it becomes an exponential equation?"

"Yes, I guess you are right."

Papa thinks for a minute, then says, "That is really something."

Trust Papa to like it when he can see it in mathematical terms!

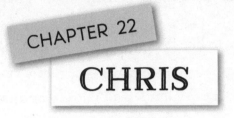

CHAPTER 22

CHRIS

I'M SHOOTING HOOPS with Diego and Trevor in my driveway when Karina comes over waving the *Lonestar Times*. She folds it open and hands it to me. There's a big photo of the memorial.

Diego reads the caption under the photograph out loud: "*Hope and love fight hate. The students of Spring Hill Middle School lead the way in demonstrating how tolerance can fight hate. The kids are all right.*"

We all stand there and grin at each other.

"Ashley is going to love this," says Karina. She takes a picture and sends it to Ashley. "And, guys, I just called Mrs. Maxwell to thank her. I'm going to meet her at the memorial. Ashley's coming too. Y'all want to come along?"

"Sure," I say, and Diego and Trevor agree.

"We can wait while you get your bike," I tell her. "We all have ours."

"Do we have to ride?" Karina asks.

When I tell her it'll be fun, she gives me a funny look but goes to get her bike.

Diego, Trevor, and I are on our bikes waiting when Karina comes pedaling out of her garage. She raises her chin and shoots us a look, defying us to say anything.

Her bike is Barbie pink—all glittery and tasseled. It was probably a perfect fit when she was like eight.

She points to the unicorn stickers on the handlebars, and then we all crack up. None of us can stop laughing.

"Lastly," she says, and turns her bike around, "behold the rhinestone-studded license plate with my name. It was my seventh-birthday present. I stopped riding it a few years ago and, obviously, never bothered to get a new one."

"Man," I say, "I'll never complain about inheriting Matt's old stuff again."

☆

Ashley's in front of the school when we arrive. We stop at the playground so we can shoot a few hoops while we wait for Mrs. Maxwell to show up.

The girls sit on the swings, and after a few shots, Diego drops the ball to join them. "When I was a kid, I was a king on the swings," he says with a straight face.

"The 'swing king' has a ring to it," Karina says with a half smile.

"The swing king is a thing?" says Ashley, getting in on the rhymefest.

"Did the swing king sing?" Trevor says, and bursts into song.

How can I resist? I'm drawn to the peals of laughter, and I race over and grab a swing.

I think it's been years since any of us have played on the swing set. But we haven't forgotten how, and we push off from the wood chips and pump our feet.

Ashley makes Diego a crown of leaves and tells him it'll be years till he lives down the swing king title.

We're the only ones on the playground, and it feels so good to act like we're six years old—back when the only monsters we knew were villains in fairy tales and video games.

☆

When it's time to meet Mrs. Maxwell, we head over to the memorial.

A group of sixth graders is just leaving, and when they spy Karina, they wave. Then some eighth graders who are hanging by the fence give us a thumbs-up.

"You know them?" Diego says in awe.

"Not personally, dude," I say. "But I guess we all know each other a little bit now because of Karina's pictures."

"Yeah, that's cool," Diego says.

Mrs. Maxwell arrives, waving the paper, and Ashley gets a look at it.

Karina introduces Mrs. Maxwell to Ashley, Diego, and Trevor. "This was their idea," she tells Mrs. Maxwell. "They started it."

"What an amazing way to show that this community stands by Mr. Chopra, Karina, and Chris," Mrs. Maxwell says. She has us all stand by the memorial for a picture and promises to send it to Karina. Then she takes a selfie with all of us.

"Speaking of pictures, I really like what you've posted, Karina," Mrs. Maxwell says. "Your shots are so moving. Would you mind if I share one or two?"

"I don't mind," says Karina. "Sometimes, I feel like the whole world should know. Other times, I worry that my grandfather would not like it. But I think he's beginning to understand that it's important to talk about all this."

Before we leave, Karina takes a picture of Mrs. Maxwell, me, Diego, Trevor, and Ashley against the pink streaks in the sky.

In the evening, Karina posts it online with the caption **Friends**. And I love her hashtags: **#GoodPeople, #GoodDay, #HateHasNoHomeHere**.

CHAPTER 23

KARINA

AT THE REHAB center, a staff member points Mom, Dad, and me to a room. "He's in a physical therapy session," she says. "If he doesn't want you there, he'll let you know and you can wait out here. He's had a rough night, which is not unusual at this point."

Papa is walking between two railings. He faces away from us. A physical therapist hovers as he takes each step.

As we walk in, we hear Papa saying, "I am too tired. Let me take a break today."

It's the first time I have heard Papa say something like this. The physical therapist brings the wheelchair and lets him sit.

When the physical therapist sees us, he wheels Papa over. "Your family is here, Mr. Chopra. Why don't you visit with them, and then we'll reassess."

I greet Papa with a hug and he smiles, but his smile does not seem wholehearted. It doesn't reach his eyes.

Dad wheels Papa out to the courtyard. It's October, and finally getting a little cooler.

"You didn't sleep well?" Dad asks.

Papa nods but does not say a word. I'm not used to him being low-energy. He's the one who gives the rest of us pep talks.

Mom moves her chair closer to Papa and holds his hands. "Papa," she says, "I have some important news."

The urgency in her voice surprises us all. It's as if she is willing Papa to listen.

"Trisha?" Dad says, but Mom doesn't even look at him.

"Papa, I know it is hard, but you have to keep going and getting stronger," Mom tells him. "You have to be there to greet your new grandchild."

I look at Mom like she has lost her marbles. Is she lying to give Papa hope?

I glance over at Dad, and now he is grinning.

"Papa," Dad says, "did you hear that?"

Papa smiles, and this time it transforms his face. "Of course I did."

"We wanted to wait till Trisha was safely at three months to share the news," Dad says, putting his arm around Mom. "We are almost there—a few days away."

I can't believe my ears. *What? Mom is pregnant?*

Not that I'm not excited or anything—I have always wanted a sibling. When I was five, I asked Santa for one. I promised Mom that I would be the best big sister in the universe. When I was seven, I said I would give up my American Girl doll, the one that looked like me, if I had a baby sister instead. Slowly, though, I understood that it was not to be, and by the time I was around eight I stopped asking.

Now I think back and remember Mom feeling sick a lot this past month. She wasn't really sick; she was pregnant, and it was nausea.

Papa holds Mom's hand and says, "I promise I will work harder than I have ever worked before."

The physical therapist returns and tells Papa that they can call it a day if he is tired.

"No," he says. "I need to work harder. I have a new grandchild on the way. I need to be walking before that baby arrives."

On my way out, I hold my mom's hand. She squeezes back. We both giggle.

Many years ago, on my one and only trip to India, I rode a camel. It was sitting on the beach, and my cousin and I climbed a ladder to get on it. We were told to hold on when the camel rose to its feet. As it got up, it lurched and rocked up and down before it straightened itself out. To five-year-old me, it was like being on an animal roller coaster.

That's what life feels like right now. The ups and downs are making me dizzy.

☆

At night, I can't fall asleep. I read all the messages of support on social media till my eyes cross. *Hang in there,* everyone says.

By three in the morning, I am still awake. The light of the almost-full moon streams in through the slats of my blinds. I toss and turn, and can't help worrying about what will happen if Papa is not able to walk independently again. What would that mean to our family?

But I cannot allow myself to go there. He must get better.

I get up and find the album of Papa's old pictures that we brought back home. I find the photograph of Papa and Grandma standing in front of their sweet little blue house, with the marigolds blooming.

They have the biggest smiles on their faces. Their lawn is perfectly manicured, and there is a garland of flowers on the front door. Their beaming faces say they have made it. After years of hard work and jumping through every immigration hoop, they had achieved their dream. They had a place of their own. Papa said it had felt like a palace.

I keep staring at the picture. I take a photo of it and try to find the right words.

Finally, I type, **What does an American look like? #Immigrants, #WeBelong, #IAmAmerican.**

Then I add **#CountMeIn,** and I post it.

CHAPTER 24

CHRIS

RAIN LASHING AGAINST my window wakes me up earlier than usual. When I look out at the street, it's like there's a river flowing.

I pick up my phone to check the time and see if Karina has posted anything new. She has.

I can barely recognize Mr. C—he looks so young in the picture that Karina has shared. Then I read the hashtags, and I literally fall back on my bed. **#CountMeIn**. Whoa!

I want to post a photo with that hashtag too. I scramble around in my room to find the picture I need.

It's one of my great-grandpa, with his sandy-blond hair, in his overalls, riding his tractor in the wheat fields of Nebraska. **#CountMeIn**. I tag Karina and Mrs. Maxwell.

Mom has woken up. I can hear her putzing around in the kitchen, and soon I smell coffee. "Chris," she calls. "Did you see the text from the school?"

School has been delayed this morning, due to flooding on some of the low-lying streets like ours. Buses can't run their routes. Instead of the bus coming as usual at 7:20 a.m., it will come at ten.

After a celebratory dance around the kitchen, I text Karina. She has already heard about the late school opening and invites me over.

"Is that your grandfather?" she asks as I walk in her door. She saw my post.

"My great-grandfather," I say.

"I love it," she says.

"Karina, do you think the rain might have ruined the tree memorial?"

"I sure hope not," she says.

The doorbell rings, and Karina's mom peeks out. "It's Mrs. Maxwell," she tells us, surprised.

Karina's mom opens the door, and Mrs. Maxwell walks in wearing a raincoat.

Mrs. Maxwell gestures to a colossal F-150 Raptor parked outside. "I borrowed it from my neighbor to safely drive through the water," she says. "Have y'all seen what's happening?"

Mrs. Maxwell opens her phone and shows us Karina's photo, which she shared on her social media. "Oh, Karina," she says. "'Count Me In'? How could I not share this picture?"

Mrs. Maxwell is not the only one who connected with it.

It has been shared. And shared.

And then shared some more.

We look at each other in disbelief.

Now pictures with #CountMeIn are coming in faster than the rain outside the window.

There's a picture of a black man with eyes as blue as the ocean.

There's one of a newborn baby, and another one of an old dude with more wrinkles than hair.

There's a picture of a Sikh man with a turban, and one of some teens wearing hijabs.

There's a picture of a man with dreadlocks down to his shoulders, another of a Chinese American family, and one of an Indian woman wearing a bindi and a sari.

There's a woman wearing a suit, a construction worker, and a kid riding his tricycle, which is decked out in red, white, and blue.

There's a picture of the El Último taco truck with the owner and his family serving a line of people.

And on and on it goes.

The shares remind me once again of the drums in the forest, beating to communicate messages in the old days.

I want to bang the drums so hard now that everyone will pay attention. I can imagine my hands thumping the skin of the drum, beating it till they turn red.

Then Karina spots pictures posted by our friends

and family—Ms. Trotter, Ashley, Diego, and Karina's mom. And, yes, even one from my dad pops up. I didn't even know my dad knew how to use social media!

Then it hits me.

This is what it means for a post to go viral.

I need to post another picture, so I put one up of the basketball team. Yes, Quinn is in it too. But there's also Diego and Trevor. We come in all shades. I tag it with #IAmAmerican, #CountMeIn.

☆

When we get to school, the first thing we notice is the tree memorial. The rain did *not* ruin it, because someone had covered it with tarp. Karina gets teary.

There's a group of students and staff in the foyer, and they all have their phones out, raised above their heads, and they're waving them at Karina. One of the kids explains that his mom saw the viral post and showed it to her. A few other kids come to high-five Karina.

Karina looks at me, shocked, like school suddenly moved to Mars or something. Then she squares her shoulders.

I grin.

She bows and waves her phone at them.

Sweet!

When I see Quinn, he tells me that I should have

asked his permission before sharing the picture of the team.

"Whatever, dude!" I say. Then I add, "Maybe you should open your eyes a little wider."

At lunchtime, I sneak into the bathroom and see that there are pictures coming in from all over—Alaska, Minnesota, Kentucky, and New York City.

It's like Karina has pushed a ball down the hill, and there's no stopping it.

On the bus ride home, Karina gets a ton of high fives. Quinn and a couple of his buddies keep their heads down—but at least they're being quiet.

When the bus turns onto our street, I see a Channel 3 van in front of Karina's house.

Karina's eyes get wide and she clutches my arm. "Chris, what should I do?"

Before we can come up with a plan, the bus screeches to a halt.

"Maybe we can ride the bus back to school," Karina says. "Why are they even here?"

I have a plan. We'll get off and walk in the opposite direction, to the park, then we'll call Karina's parents.

But then we see my mother standing at the bus stop. She hasn't met the bus since I was in third grade, but I've never been happier to see her. Mom pulls a stunned Karina to her side. The two of us shield her as we rush toward my house.

When we're almost at the door, a man by the van points to us and says, "Hey, isn't that the kid we're after?"

Mom literally shoves Karina into the house and bangs the door shut.

After calling Karina's parents, we go back to looking at all the #CountMeIn posts on our phones. We're like moths attracted to the light of the screen.

While the majority of the comments are supportive, I'm reminded again that there are other Quinns in the world.

There are some comments that say **America is for Americans**. I agree with that. I just don't understand why all the Americans must look alike.

There are people who echo all the things the monster hurled at Mr. Chopra.

There are comments that suggest that Karina and Mr. Chopra made it all up.

Karina is now sitting on the couch in our living room with big tears rolling down her face. She's overwhelmed by it all, the positive and the negative, and there's nothing I can do.

CHAPTER 25

KARINA

THE REPORTERS WILL not go away. When I looked out my window in the morning at all their vans and cars, I thought of Chris's dad a million years ago. How he was so upset at the car blocking his driveway when we had the party to celebrate Papa moving here. He must be hopping mad today, and I wouldn't blame him. I want them all to leave us alone too. Having my post go viral was cool—but being hounded by the media is not cool at all.

Yesterday, one of the local TV stations did a story on Mrs. Maxwell sharing my post and how it went viral. They reported on what happened to Papa and showed the memorial. They said my question has made others think and ask, *Who is an American? What does an American look like?*

When they called and asked if they could interview me, Dad refused. I am just a kid, he said. He does not want me on TV.

Since that segment, though, reporters continue to exhaust us with requests. Today, Dad picked me up after school and took me to work. Still, a few reporters showed up at our family's sandwich store looking for a statement.

The situation has been a help and a curse. It has brought in new customers who are curious, but has kept away some regulars who don't want to deal with the crowd.

And it is so weird to feel like prisoners in our own home.

In the evening, Dad calls lots of aunties and uncles to get advice. Then Sanjay Uncle, who is a lawyer, comes over to talk.

"This can't go on," Dad tells him.

I agree with that. I miss my anonymous life. Before all of this happened, I was a nobody. I could have worn mismatched socks every day and no one would have noticed, except Ashley. I was not someone who mattered in school. Now everyone wants to talk to me, and yesterday Ashley helped me choose outfits for the week.

I text Chris to tell him, **Sanjay Uncle says Dad should make a statement on behalf of the family.**

Dad and Mom sit at the dining room table with Sanjay Uncle, carefully picking and choosing their words.

After an hour, they have written a few sentences that say nothing about our pain and fears but put on a brave facade.

Sanjay Uncle reads them and makes a few changes. Then they step outside and face the reporters at our door.

Dad reads his statement:

"We appreciate the concern and good wishes expressed by the community since the attack involving my father, Shiv Chopra. He continues to recover in a rehabilitation facility, where we are grateful that he is under the care of an excellent medical team. We hope and pray for his recovery.

"We are also heartened by all the support from across the country that has been extended to our daughter and her friend, who were with my father that day.

"At this difficult time, we ask that the press give us the privacy to heal and carry on with our lives. Thank you all for all your support and interest in our well-being. We believe in this country!"

☆

The statement makes no difference.

The phone continues to ring with requests for interviews as our story continues to spread.

Dad paces in the living room. Mom throws up, and I'm not sure if it's because she is pregnant or because she is stressed-out.

Sanjay Uncle and Dad's hope that the story will go away and be forgotten has not happened. The president of the Indian American Association calls Dad to suggest this is an opportunity to bring attention to the rising number of hate crimes against South Asians.

After a long discussion, they decide that they'll allow me to be interviewed, and hopefully when people's curiosity is satisfied, the attention will drop off.

Even Papa is now aware of the situation. "Is there someone that we could trust to tell our story?" he says.

I think back to that day when Papa was assaulted. In my mind's eye, I see Papa fallen on the street and I see me and Chris. Then I hear that scream from Mrs. Maxwell, urgent and loud. "Henry!" she shouted before she rushed to help.

The choice is obvious.

We all agree we can count on Mrs. Maxwell.

"Yes, I like her," I say. "She understands, because she was there. She came to school to check on Chris and me. She is a reporter and she cares."

Dad calls her and puts her on speaker so we can all hear her. She says she will come over to our house later.

☆

When Mrs. Maxwell arrives, she has a man with her who will record our interview on video.

Mom and Dad have both coached me to take my time, think before I say anything, and not feel pressured to answer anything I don't want to.

Mrs. Maxwell wears a soft mauve-colored dress. It's loose and swirly and pretty. "Relax," she says. "I'm on your side."

I nod and say, "Thank you!"

When the camera rolls, she does a brief introduction about what happened that day and how she happened to be on the scene.

Then she turns to me to start the interview.

"Karina," she says, "how did the events of that day change you?"

"In every way," I say. "I had read about people being attacked before, but till it happens to someone you love, it's just another news story."

There is an ocean of feelings and thoughts that I am not able to communicate, like how vulnerable all this has made me feel. How I have often thought that Mrs. Maxwell was an angel sent to watch out for us.

"Tell us about your grandfather," she says.

I search for the words that will convey that he is the

most important person in my life, and I say what I come up with: "He came to this country fifty years ago. He loves math, and he volunteers in my school. He tutors my friend Chris, and that is why Chris was with us that day. Papa loves watching basketball. He used to live in California, and loves the Lakers. Now he is learning to love the Rockets."

"He sounds wonderful," Mrs. Maxwell says.

I feel more relaxed, and I start to forget that there is a camera in the room.

"He is," I say. "And he is going to get better, because he wants to be there when I have my new brother or sister."

Then I see Mom and Dad's startled faces. They have not shared the news with anyone except Papa, and here I am blurting it out to the world.

Oops!

I wish I could take back my words. But then Mom nods at me and gives me a thumbs-up.

Mrs. Maxwell sees all the surprised faces in the room and says, "Well! Congratulations on the upcoming addition to your family!

"What made you share your pictures of what happened on your photo feed?" Mrs. Maxwell asks.

"I wanted people to be as outraged as me at the way Papa was treated," I say. "The story needed to be told.

It's important because I love my country, but I don't like this hateful side of it. And for me, I feel I tell stories better with my pictures than with words."

"You're pretty good with words too." Mrs. Maxwell smiles wide. "What did you mean when you used the hashtag 'Count Me In'?"

I see Dad, Mom, Sanjay Uncle, and the others looking at me, waiting to hear my answer. Mrs. Maxwell's encouraging look says, *You can do this.*

I take a minute and breathe. "It means that I cannot be quiet anymore. Count on me to speak up."

My voice surprises me. It is firm.

Mrs. Maxwell grins wider. She says to me, "So you have become an accidental activist?"

Seeing my puzzled expression, Mrs. Maxwell explains. "You have become an activist, someone who speaks up, even if you didn't expect anyone outside your community to hear what you had to say."

Have I? Is this what an activist does? Do I know anyone who is an activist?

"I guess so," I say.

"Lastly," Mrs. Maxwell says, "what do you think of the memorial?"

"I love it," I say. "My friends Ashley, Diego, and Trevor started it. I've been showing my grandfather pictures of it, and I think it's helped us all."

"I thank you for sharing your story," Mrs. Maxwell says, "and I wish you and your family the best. So many of us are praying for your grandfather's recovery."

Then the man turns the camera off.

☆

Chris rushes over after seeing me on the news. "Wow," he says. "You did a great job. And how cool you're gonna have a kid brother or sister. I can't believe I had to find *that* out on TV, though."

"Me and my big mouth. I can't believe I blurted that out before Mom gave me the green light," I say. "It's fine, though—Mom is happy, and everyone is so excited."

"Yeah," Chris says. "It's awesome to have good news. I can't wait to say, 'Welcome to the world, Baby C. You've got the most awesome big sister ever!'"

CHAPTER 26

CHRIS

SO IT'S BEEN a day since Karina's interview with Mrs. Maxwell was in the paper and all over the local news. Now it seems like everyone—and their parents—knows her name and the story of what happened to us. It feels weird, but I'm glad Karina spoke out, and so's she.

"People need to know how badly Papa was treated, so they understand," she says. "It's worth dealing with the attention that brings, if it helps."

Lots of neighbors wave when they see us on our bikes after school riding to Ashley's house.

But when we pass a gray Ford Taurus, the same kind of car that the monster drove, my foot stops pedaling and I almost fall over.

Will this feeling ever go away?

It's just a mom and a kid from school who've slowed down to give us a thumbs-up.

"Karina," I say, and I blurt out the question that

has been bothering me for days. "Do you think I should have done more that day?"

She screeches to a halt, and I stop too.

Karina gets off that bike that's too small for her. She leans it against a tree.

"Chris Daniels," she says. "Do you remember that he had a knife?"

"I do," I say. That knife still glints in my nightmares. "Maybe I could have kicked it out of his hand?"

"Chris, come on, now. It was not a video game."

"I know, but still, I wonder what I could have done," I tell her.

"Nothing. We were all shocked, stunned. We were on a safe street. It should not have happened. But Papa told me that sometimes bad things happen to good people."

"Are you saying that to make me feel better?"

"I would never do that," she says, and puts her hand on her heart. "You have been there for me every day since then. You could have gone your own way."

"I'd never do that to people I care about," I say. "Never." I place my hand on my heart.

"I know," she says, "and that's what makes you such a great friend."

"Karina, I'm sorry about sixth grade," I confess. "I didn't stand up for you then."

"I'm sorry about sixth grade too. I used to call you and your friends 'a pack of hyenas.'"

"You did?" I say.

"Yes, but you know I don't think *you* are one anymore!"

"I don't know why I ever thought hanging with those guys would make me cool, help me survive," I tell her. "But I'm glad there's a world of kids not like them."

Karina laughs. "Me too. And that was *such* a long time ago, Chris."

"Almost so long ago that your blinged-up bike was styling, right?"

She sticks her tongue out, and I feel lighter as we get back on our bikes.

"Hey," I say as we ride off. "Which picture did you choose to submit for the contest?"

I'm surprised when she ignores my question—and she rides faster when I repeat it.

"You know you can't lose me on your bike!" I yell.

"Isn't that a shame!" she says.

When we're in front of Ashley's house, she finally answers. "I didn't choose a picture, okay?"

I raise my brows as high as they can get.

"It all seemed like too much, to choose a picture and a frame and a caption. With everything that happened, it just felt like more than I could do."

"Ashley or I could help."

She parks her bike and starts to walk up to the house.

"I thought you wanted to be in that art gallery more than anything, Karina."

She turns around. "You want the truth? I missed the deadline."

I get off my bike and park it. Karina looks miserable. Then it occurs to me. "Hey, Karina," I say, "why don't you go to the gallery and beg? Tell them what happened. They'll understand."

She looks at me like I'm nuts. "They're not going to listen to some kid whine."

"But they might listen to a kid who is an accidental activist, right?" I grin.

"Hmm, I don't know, Chris," she says, and I can hear hope creeping into her voice. "I guess it's worth a try, and if I succeed, I won't have to tell Papa that I missed the deadline, despite him reminding me."

When Ashley comes to the door, Karina tells her our plan. Then she looks at me. "Chris, you're coming with me, right?"

"Of course," I say.

"Good luck," Ashley shouts as we get back on our bikes. "And knock 'em dead!"

The gallery is a little over a mile from my house. This time we pedal in sync down the winding tree-lined streets. I have no idea if this plan will work, but I am praying for Karina, and I'm sure that she's doing the same. With her help, I've managed to hang in there with my math grades so that I don't disappoint Mr. Chopra. Karina cannot fail him either.

We arrive at the gallery and park our bikes. The silver sign at the entrance reads CONTEMPORARY ARTS AND CRAFTS.

I rush up to the door and see that they close at five thirty. It is just five thirty now. Karina and I push the front door, and nothing happens. We knock; nothing happens. Desperate, I shake it, as if that will somehow open it.

We are about to give up and leave when an older girl in overalls opens the big glass door and a gust of cold air greets us. "Did you need something?" she asks.

"Yes!" Karina says eagerly. "We're so glad you are still here."

"I'm Riley, the assistant," the girl tells us. "The owner—my boss—has gone home."

Karina extends her hand and introduces herself, and I do the same.

"Well, come on in," Riley says, and we follow her into a large room with polished wood floors. Our footsteps echo. The room is empty except for the huge paintings on the walls.

Riley sits down, and tells us to as well. "How can I help you?" she asks.

Karina takes a deep breath and says, "I am a photographer, and I have always wanted to enter your competition."

"The deadline was two days ago," Riley says.

"I know," Karina says, and takes another deep breath.

I jump in. "Karina's been talking about this forever, and if her grandfather hadn't been in the hospital, she would have been the first one to send in her pictures."

"Oh!" Riley says. "Is that true?"

Karina stands up. "I shouldn't have come. I knew the deadline was the day before yesterday. I don't know what I was thinking."

"I hope you enter next year," Riley says. She keeps staring at Karina. "You look familiar. Have you taken a class with us before?"

"No, I haven't."

Riley stares some more and snaps her fingers. "I've got it! I read about you in the paper, didn't I? You were the kids who were attacked with your grandfather."

"We were," Karina says.

"Mr. Chopra was in the hospital, and now he's in rehab. He had a fractured femur," I say. "That's the bone in his thigh."

Riley's eyes are wide. "Ouch!"

"He's learning to walk all over again," Karina says. "If it wasn't for that, I would never have missed the deadline."

"I'm so sorry," Riley says. "I'd like to help you. I'll talk to my boss. Why don't you come back tomorrow? Bring your photograph, and maybe that will sway Margaret's mind."

Karina and I leave with the biggest smiles.

"There's no way that her boss will say no," I tell Karina. "She'd have to have no heart if she refused."

☆

In the evening, I read Mrs. Maxwell's article again online. Then I make the mistake of reading the comments. Matt's told me so many times not to read people's dumb comments on stuff. *That's like poking through the garbage,* he's said.

Most of the comments are supportive, but there are plenty that aren't. Folks who spew trash from accounts with names like Whitehope15.

I call Karina to tell her that her interview with Mrs. Maxwell is online.

"I know," she says.

"Promise me not to read the comments."

"Dad made me promise that too," she says.

"This is important. Please don't," I say. "Please?"

CHAPTER 27

KARINA

EVERY PHOTO FROM my "Worth Keeping" folder is laid out in my room, till every surface is covered, even the floor. Walking requires me to tiptoe around moments from my life. They are all the objects and people that attracted my eye and made me zoom in with my camera.

There is the stone river that meanders through Ashley's backyard. The blue bench that I saw in Maine. The wisteria climbing on a fence in a desolate neighborhood. A purple front door propped open an inch. Dogs of all shapes and sizes, because I want one.

I look from one photo to the other. They are all pretty. Beautiful even. But none feels right.

I call Ashley and fill her in on the happenings at the art gallery.

She comes over and stands at the door to my room. "Whoa! What in the world, Karina?"

"On your tippy-toes, Ash," I say.

She enters, and does the Ashley thing. She surveys

all the photos, and I am quiet as can be. Then Ashley stares at the pics for a while longer, closes her eyes, and picks.

It has worked in the past.

This time, Ashley picks the photo of the door. "I love the way it is open just a bit. I don't know what's inside, but I want to push it open."

I pick it up and peer at it closely. "You think so?"

I put it down and pick up another one.

"These pictures were all taken by the *old* me," I say.

Ashley raises her brows. "That is still you."

"It is, and it isn't."

I feel like a new Karina now that hate has become three-dimensional for me. Since the attack, my story has changed.

A half hour later, after a few more suggestions I don't take, I can see that Ashley is frustrated.

I can't blame her. I am losing patience with myself.

After she leaves, I take a break from my room with all its pictures. I open my phone and look at the pictures that people continue to post with the #CountMeIn hashtag.

These are the pictures that make me happy now, less alone. I am looking at a picture of two little best friends. They remind me of me and Ashley in third grade.

I close my eyes tight. In my mind, I see all the pictures that have been shared over the last few days. Instead of being on the screen of my phone, they are all framed and they hang on the pristine walls of the art gallery with spotlights illuminating them.

I keep my eyes closed tight, because *that* is the exhibition I want to see. I want the whole world to see. But I can enter only one picture, not hundreds.

Then I check out Mrs. Maxwell's article online. I promised Dad and Chris that I would not look at the comments—I know they just want to spare me further pain—but I go there anyway. I have read negative comments before, with a hashtag some jerk started called #CountMeOut.

It's like opening Pandora's box.

The majority are supportive, offering love and support. But the negative ones sting like a hundred fire ants on a Texas summer day.

Whitehope15 says: Americans are white and Christian.

Angryman says: We don't want no Arabs here.

OriginalAryan says: They are robbing the system, these brown people. Do they even have jobs?

Realcitizen says: I don't believe a word any of these people say. They need to all go back.

There are others. They can be hateful on the internet because no one knows who they are.

I slap my laptop shut and stare at it as if I have trapped a rat in there.

I go outside and stare at the night sky. The waning moon is milky white. The stars feel especially bright tonight, like they are speaking to me and urging me on. I feel my heart pounding. I feel the breeze on my face. I keep seeing all the pictures. My mind races from one picture to another and matches my heartbeat. I keep staring at the stars till all the pictures in my head blur and become one.

☆

Mom drops me off to visit Papa in the morning. He takes one look at my face and asks, "What's the matter, Karina?"

"Why is there so much hate in the world?" I say.

"Come here," he says, and pats his bed. "There is good and evil in this world. There always has been, there always will be. You know there is a constant struggle between love and hate."

"I do?" I say.

Papa reminds me of the stories he read to me about those battles—with the churning of seas, the serpents emerging from the ocean, and the lightning bolts from the sky. Together we've read stories of the battles between Harry Potter and Voldemort, and between Rama and Ravana.

With patience, Papa reminds me that evil exists everywhere, in every corner and every country on Earth—but so does good.

"We can't stop fighting for good," I say.

The physical therapist arrives for Papa's walking practice. Papa takes painful steps all over again, but he has his mojo back.

"Mr. Chopra, you have amazed me this week," the physical therapist says. "You can do this, right?"

"Oh, I can!" Papa proclaims. "I have a new grandchild on the way that I have to chase. I have to work harder, but I have been doing that all my life. Nothing new."

☆

On the drive home, I am quiet. My thoughts whip around like the trees in a storm.

Having seen the dark side of the world on the internet, I know that it is even more important to fight for love, and to find the silver light. To make Papa proud.

The first thing I do is gather all the pictures in my room, put them in neat piles and manila envelopes, and put them away. I am going to need every clear surface to accomplish what I imagine. And help.

I call Chris, then Ashley, to tell them I need their help, and they are both over in a few minutes.

They help me choose pictures from the hundreds that have been posted with the hashtag #CountMeIn.

"We need to pick some from the hashtag 'Count Me Out' too," I say.

They wrinkle their noses. "Do we have to?" Ashley says.

"You know we do," I say.

"You don't want to leave out anyone, not even the haters?" says Ashley.

"No. Because they make the whole," says Chris. "The good and the evil."

I upload the pictures to the drugstore website to be printed. It will take an hour.

"Do you have the money to pay for it?" asks Chris.

I have been saving all my birthday money for years to buy a camera, but this is bigger than that. "Yes, I have it covered," I say.

Then we head out on our bikes to the office-supply place. We buy extra-large foam poster board. Two boards in case we mess up. But we can't balance the boards on our bikes and ride safely.

Chris calls his brother, who is home for a visit. Matt comes to our rescue and drives to the store to pick up the foam boards.

Ashley has to take off, but Chris, Matt, and I head back home, and I grab my colored pencils and bring them next door. I decide to get Matt's help drawing the outline of the East Coast. Matt is a history major—and good at art—and will do a better job of all the squiggly little lines. I would hate to mess it up and cut off Delaware.

"Did your grandfather come to America in the sixties?" he asks me.

"He did," I say. "1968. Wait, how do you know that?"

"Because I'm studying immigration," he says. "And the Immigration Act of 1965 allowed lots of people with skills to come here from Asia, Africa, and the Middle East."

"How was it before?" I ask.

"In the fifties and earlier, there was a quota system," Matt tells us, "which favored people from Europe."

"Wow!" I say. "I need to talk to Papa about that."

I wish I had more time to talk to Matt, but I have this poster to finish.

I have a few hours to put my thoughts and my feelings onto this poster.

Chris helps, but there is only so much he can do. I *feel* this project more than I know it. Putting it into words is difficult even though I know how I want it to look at the end.

So I snip and cut with my scissors. With all the focus I can summon, I piece together the puzzle. I cut small pieces, and others that are bigger. I want to try to get in as many of the five-hundred-plus pictures that were posted as I can. I start placing them onto the board, inside the outline of the map.

Soon, photo by clipped photo, the map starts filling in, like brushstrokes on an empty canvas. The collage is coming together. I squint my eyes, stand at a distance, and stare at it till it all melds into one beautiful whole.

Chris is quiet for a bit. Then he says, "This is the most amazing thing ever, Karina."

"Not yet, Chris," I say, because I can see I need to move pictures around. The balance is off. There are too many men in the right corner and too many people wearing blue on the left.

Finally, I have the photos all laid out and in place.

The space in the center is blank, but Chris and I both know which picture goes there. The picture of Papa and Grandma, with their first house, where they stare into the camera as if they are daring the world to give them a chance. I wonder if Papa dreamed that day that he would have an American granddaughter who would want to speak up for him.

I clip the new print I got of the photo into the shape of a star, and I place it in the center of the collage. It feels like placing the last and most important piece in a thousand-piece puzzle.

Now I must glue them all in place so I can take it to the art gallery to show the boss lady.

Chris says what I am thinking as I marvel at the finished poster: "How could she refuse to display this?"

"I hope she can't," I say. "This is all of us."

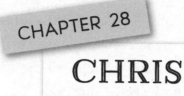

CHAPTER 28

CHRIS

MATT DRIVES US to the art gallery and waits in the car.

Riley greets Karina with hugs and crossed fingers. She introduces us to her boss, Margaret.

"Thank you for seeing us," Karina says. "I am so excited to show you my work."

Karina and I turn the board around and hold it up.

Margaret stands. She peers and squints like Karina and I did.

Finally, Margaret says, "You can put it down."

She sits back at her desk, fiddles with a pen, and clears her throat.

"Karina," Margaret says. "Honey, I love this."

Karina breaks into a smile.

Then Margaret stands, clears her throat again, and says, "But I'm sorry, I can't make an exception to the rules. You see, it wouldn't be fair to those who did submit their entries on time."

What? After all Karina's been through, this makes no sense.

I look over at Karina. The smile has disappeared.

"You see, Riley meant well," Margaret says, "but she didn't know that I went through all the submissions yesterday morning and chose the ones we wanted to exhibit for every category. I already sent out confirmation emails to the winners. If I made an exception for you, I would have to drop someone after having already informed them that they're in."

Now Karina looks like she's struggling not to cry.

Margaret puts her hand on Karina's shoulder. "I cannot tell you how sorry I am. I wish there was more space on our walls."

I want to scream, *Figure it out. Place it on an easel and put it in the middle of the room. Put it on the ceiling. Michelangelo painted on the ceilings. People will look up.*

As we leave, Margaret says, "Karina, I hope you will enter next time."

Karina nods, but her face is a blank canvas.

As we step out, Riley comes running out from the back. It's clear she can tell it did not go well, and she squeezes Karina's hand. "I'm so sorry," she says. "I'm following your posts."

One look at us, and Matt can tell what happened too.

On the drive home, we are all quiet. Sometimes there

is just nothing to say. Karina stares out of the window. The radio announcer is all cheerful, talking about Halloween costume ideas and pumpkins and candy corn. Like anybody cares.

☆

Mom makes Matt's favorite dinner—spaghetti and meatballs—which is usually my favorite too. But tonight, I'm not that hungry.

After dinner, Matt suggests we go outside to look at the stars. "It's gonna be a spectacle tonight."

I text Karina to join us, so then there we are, the three of us in my backyard, looking up at the darkening sky.

"Chris, Karina," Matt says, "I'm proud of you both. I know it hasn't been easy."

Karina sighs and mumbles, "Thank you."

"It's been hard in so many ways," I say, and I tell Matt about the internet comments.

"Let them go," he says. "They are on the wrong side of history. This country is way more diverse than it was in the fifties, and no one can turn back time."

Soon, the light has faded completely, and the stars emerge like actors on a stage.

Karina points to the brightest. "That must be the star everyone wishes upon."

"Nope," Matt says. "That's actually a planet—it's Venus."

Then Matt points to another bright object by its side. "And ta-da! That's Mercury. Typically, it's faint and hard to see, but Venus shining nearby makes it visible."

Being near Venus makes Mercury visible. I like that. It makes me think how being Karina's friend has made me stronger.

"Karina, if I had a wish," I say, "it'd be that I owned that art gallery. I would make room for your poster."

"For real," Matt says. "Karina's poster is our America."

I swear a star drops when he says that.

CHAPTER 29

KARINA

MOM TAKES ONE look at what Chris calls my "sad-sack face" and insists that she needs help at work. I would rather stay at home and mope around. But Dad is at the rehab center this morning, and you can't refuse when your pregnant mom asks for help. That's a no-no.

I get put to work chopping and filling the vegetable bins. Onions, cucumbers, banana peppers, olives, spinach, lettuce, tomatoes. All the basic toppings for sandwiches.

Mom is still fielding calls from friends and family about Papa, about me being on the news, and of course about the miracle baby. No one can believe that Mom is pregnant after all these years!

I hear her cutting off a conversation with her aunt. "I am busy at the store, but Papa is up and walking and truly on the mend," she says.

Instead of dumping the sliced cucumbers into their

bin, I find myself arranging them in pretty patterns. It is soothing.

"Karina," Mom calls from her office in the back of the store. "Are you done with the vegetables?"

I am done with the cucumbers, and they are a work of art. I hustle to get the rest of the vegetables ready with no fuss.

I hear Mom's phone go off again—her ringtone is a song from the Bollywood film *Kal Ho Naa Ho*.

"What?" I hear her say. "How? When?"

She sounds frantic. "What time will you be home?"

I race over. What's happening?

Mom hangs up and leans against the bench seat, cradling her tummy, which has popped out in the last few days. My brother or sister is growing fast.

"Papa is coming home," she says.

"On Monday, I know," I say, heading back to my job in the kitchen. "That's a good thing—why the twenty questions?"

"Karina," Mom says, "he's coming home today. Later this afternoon."

"What?" I say.

But it makes sense. Papa was so much better when I visited last.

Turns out the doctor went to see him this morning and said to Dad that Papa looked great, and why keep him there in the rehab place the whole weekend? He ordered the staff to get everything done today and release him for discharge this afternoon.

Mom, Dad, and I had counted on having tonight to get everything ready.

"Mom," I said, "I wanted to have a homecoming party for Papa."

"I know you did," she says, "and I wanted one too. But there's no time today."

Mom calls Lisa and Amit, who both work at the store, and tells them what's going on. They rush over so that Mom and I can go home.

Back at the house, we assess the situation. Fortunately, Dad and his friends have already cleared out the den to make room for Papa's bed, since Papa can't climb stairs yet. Mom gets the linens to make the bed up, and I bring down some of Papa's photos and books.

I make a sign that says WELCOME HOME, PAPA! and Mom helps me color it and add glitter.

I think back to the party we had to welcome Papa to Houston, when Chris hesitantly walked into our lives. That seems like a lifetime ago.

I text Chris to let him know Papa is coming home today, and in a minute he is over at my house, whooping and cheering.

"There's no time to plan a party," Chris says. "So how can we make it special?"

"I'm not sure," I say.

"Has Mr. C seen the heart memorial?" he asks.

"Only in pictures," I say.

"So let's ask your dad to take him there on the way home," Chris says, and we high-five at his brilliant idea.

Then I have an aha moment. "That's where the poster needs to be," I say.

"OMG! Why did we even bother with the art gallery?" Chris says. "Let's do it!"

Chris and I make plans, and I tell him I will let him know the time frame for Papa's arrival at the memorial after I confirm everything with my dad.

I can feel the excitement building now. This will be the homecoming Papa deserves.

Papa already knows about the tree memorial—he got teary-eyed when I filled him in on it, and said, "You have good friends, Karina. Hold on to them."

"Papa," I told him, "it's as much for you as it is for me."

"I want to thank every one of them for making me feel like I belong," he said. "Do you know how long it took to feel like this was truly my country? It feels good to be told over and over again that I do belong."

So, yes, Papa needs to see the tree on his way home.

I call Dad, who is not sure at first. Fortunately, Mom picks up the phone and says, "Jay, he will feel good. It will help him to slowly forget the hate he received before. You can pull up in the car right next to the memorial."

I am so happy when Dad agrees and says they will probably arrive at the tree a little after five. Papa, he reports, is full of energy and excited to be going home.

Then Mom calls Mrs. Kumar, who calls a few other friends, and they all agree to meet us at the tree.

I post a picture of the WELCOME HOME, PAPA! sign and write: **Papa comes home today. I want him to see all the flowers and messages that you all have placed on the tree near school. We are going to take him there around 5:00 pm. I want him to feel the love #SayNoToHate, #HateHasNoHomeHere, #WeBelong, #CountMeIn.**

Matt drives us and the poster to the memorial to wait for Papa.

Chris and I tidy up the flowers. We make sure there is nothing hateful around. I know there will always be Quinns and other haters in the world, but I won't tolerate it right now.

Ashley, Diego, and Trevor arrive. We marvel at the number of green heart leaves people have hung on the tree.

Mom comes with Mrs. Kumar and a few other friends. There are now about ten of us. I take pictures.

We lean the collage up against the tree.

Mom studies it once again and smiles. Her beaming face is like the rainbow after a stormy afternoon day. Then she brushes away tears.

Ashley takes a picture. Our little party of supporters is ready for Papa.

CHAPTER 30

CHRIS

INVITE THEM, AND they will come.

A little before five, cars and bikes start rolling in. Even with all the attention that her posts have gotten, Karina didn't expect this kind of turnout.

There are kids from school and our neighborhood who know Karina and me—and tons of others who don't but still want to show they have our backs.

My parents show up with flowers.

Ms. Trotter comes with shiny balloons. Anne Maxwell arrives with her husband. Even Riley from the art gallery shows up.

Everyone's drawn to Karina's poster. So many of the people who posted pictures with the #CountMeIn hashtag are here today, and they look and find themselves in the collage.

Karina walks around thanking them all.

The crowd continues to grow.

"Wow, that's Papa's senior-citizen group from the

temple," Karina says, pointing to a group of older men and women who are walking toward us. Her mom rushes over to greet them.

"It's been just over two weeks since that day, and it was around this time," I say to Karina.

She nods. "So much has changed, hasn't it?"

"For sure." The time might be the same as that day when hate blindsided us, but nothing else is similar. Today, we're surrounded by only good people.

At five fifteen, Karina begins to worry. "Chris," she says. "Why aren't they here yet?"

I can see her mom looking anxiously at her watch too. Karina calls her dad, and the phone rings and rings and then goes to voicemail.

"Karina," I say, "your dad never answers the phone when he's driving."

And, sure enough, a minute later we see his car drive up—followed by a TV news van.

Karina's dad parks, pop the trunk, and takes out a walker. The TV news van parks, and the videographer positions himself in minutes.

Karina's dad and my dad help Mr. Chopra out of the car. He leans on his walker and looks stunned—by the people, the hearts, the love. While he has known about the attention his story has received, he was isolated in rehab. He was probably focused more on being able to live and stand and walk.

Slowly Mr. C walks over to the tree.

He calls me and Karina to his side. We stand on either side of him. The original three friends.

The camera phones click.

Mr. C examines the poster closely, pointing in wonderment to the people he knows. He points to his own picture in the middle of the poster, in the heart of the map. "Me?" he says.

Karina smiles at him. "Yes, you!" she says.

Mr. C seems to be searching for the right words. He shakes his head as if he can't believe this is happening.

Then he begins to speak to the crowd. "Thank you for making me feel like I belong. I am an immigrant, and India will always be dear to me. But I have lived in this country for fifty years—I made a home, raised my family, and paid taxes."

People chuckle.

"I am an old man. I have learned that there are people who do good things and some who do bad. It has nothing to do with your religion or skin color. I am lucky to be surrounded by all you good people."

Karina has tears in her eyes, and I feel like I might start bawling.

"I am proud to be an American," Mr. C continues in a shaky voice. "I don't know hashtags and social media, but . . . Karina, how do you say it?"

Karina says, "Count me in."

"Count me in," he says.

Someone says, "I belong. You belong."

Someone else says, "Say no to hate."

Then someone repeats, "Count me in."

And one by one, people echo, "Count me in," till that is all we can hear.

CHAPTER 31

KARINA

THAT EVENING, WE celebrate, even though we all know Papa still has a long road to regaining his strength ahead.

We don't let the anonymous haters on the internet stop us from admiring the collage and taking a photo. I post a picture of it and tag it **#AllOfUs**, **#America**, **#StrongerTogether**.

That evening, Mom lines up flour, butter, sugar, and eggs—just like on a cooking show—and bakes a cake. Not any old cake, but the one from Grandma's recipe that Papa loves. The cake we were supposed to bake when Chris got an A and my picture was accepted in the art gallery, but Papa's homecoming is more special than any of that.

I whip the cream to beautiful stiff, frothy peaks. When the cake is done, Mom will frost it and I will pile it high with berries.

And I really can't believe it when Mom says, "Who wants dessert for dinner?"

What? What? What?

"Yes! Yes! Yes!" I say.

When the cake is ready, we sit outside under a starry sky with our dinner-size slices.

For a moment, when I see the strawberries, I am reminded of the splattered ones from that day.

And it's as if Papa reads my mind. Softly, he says, "One berry, two berry."

Immediately, he transports me to a safer place. Once again, he shows me how to not let fear and anger win.

"One berry, two berry," I say. "Welcome home, Papa Bear-y."

"Karina," Dad says, "I hope you've saved that book to read to the baby."

"No worries. I have," I say. "It's a special edition, with a few bonus banana stains."

As the sky darkens, we all look up at Venus, sparkling like a magical jewel.

Papa points to it and tells Chris, "Maybe when I tutor you tomorrow, we will calculate the distance to Venus, Earth's sister planet."

Papa is wasting no time getting back to work, I am happy to see.

"We used to call Venus the evening star," Papa says. "If I could wish upon it, it would be for continued healing—and a peaceful future with my family and all my new friends."

"Me too, Papa," I tell him. "I'm counting on that."

"I hear you, Mr. C," Chris says. "And a future with a Lakers versus Rockets game, and more cake-for-dinner parties too."

Papa's laugh is loud and deep.

I might have once thought that Chris Daniels and I were separate planets orbiting in the same galaxy, but today I am glad that we are friends wishing upon the same star.

AUTHOR'S NOTE

I landed in St. Louis, Missouri, in the fall of 1986 to attend graduate school. In 1987, I remember being at an international student night, which was attended by students from over fifty countries. It was my first exposure to such heady diversity, and I was hooked.

Upon completion of my degree, armed with youthful optimism, I decided to work and stay in St. Louis. I've had the good fortune to be raised and nurtured by both India and America.

My husband and I met during those years, and we married in a Hindu ceremony at the nondenominational religious center on the university campus. The center had a glass dome roof etched with the world map. It felt so appropriate and fitting.

Some of my dearest and closest friends are immigrants.

This country has been built by immigrant dreams and has flourished with our ambition.

I write this author's note a day after an incident has occurred in my own community. A Muslim resident's house was shot at, and the police are investigating it as a possible hate crime.

The resident shared the experience on the community Facebook page. The response from the community was swift, caring, compassionate, and intolerant of hate. There were offers of prayers. There were offers of support, solidarity, and help. Some wanted to start a fund to help pay for the damage to the house. Among all that support, there was an opinion voiced that reminded me that we have much work to do.

The incidence of hate has risen not just in America but all around the world.

It will take all of us working together to find a way forward, just like Karina and Chris.

ACKNOWLEDGMENTS

While the author's name appears on the cover, it takes a village to create a book.

Many have helped me in my journey.

My paternal grandfather read Jane Austen sitting on his rocking chair in the verandah at Shanti Niwas. My father introduced me to photography and Indian classical music. My mother inculcated in me the discipline essential to see a project to completion.

I would like to thank a benevolent universe for giving me the opportunity to work with Nancy Paulsen. Her guidance was always gentle and nurturing. Her thoughtful, intelligent, and insightful comments and questions were invaluable.

Sara LaFleur, Elizabeth Johnson, Cindy Howle, and the rest of the team at Penguin, thank you for your attention to every detail. You're the best.

My critique partners and fellow quiche and scone eaters, Laura Ruthven and Crystal Allen, made me dig deep and wouldn't let me settle for anything short of the truth. Thank you so much.

My agent, Jill Corcoran, believed in the story and made sure that I told it in a way that held the reader's interest.

Anne Bustard, my beta reader, dropped everything and made time for me.

Dr. Maya Mayekar, Dr. Nirica Borges, and Dr. Emily Mayekar helped me portray Papa's injuries realistically.

Law enforcement experts answered my questions with patience.

Eleni Kalorkoti's cover art captures the spirit of the story.

Cynthia Leitich Smith and Kathi Appelt have encouraged and guided by example over the years.

I owe gratitude to Rajeev, Samir, and Karishma for supporting my passion, and to Scamper, who is by my side every day as I commit words to the page.